DANCE ME A DARK-HAIRED BEAUTY

TESSA MCFIONN

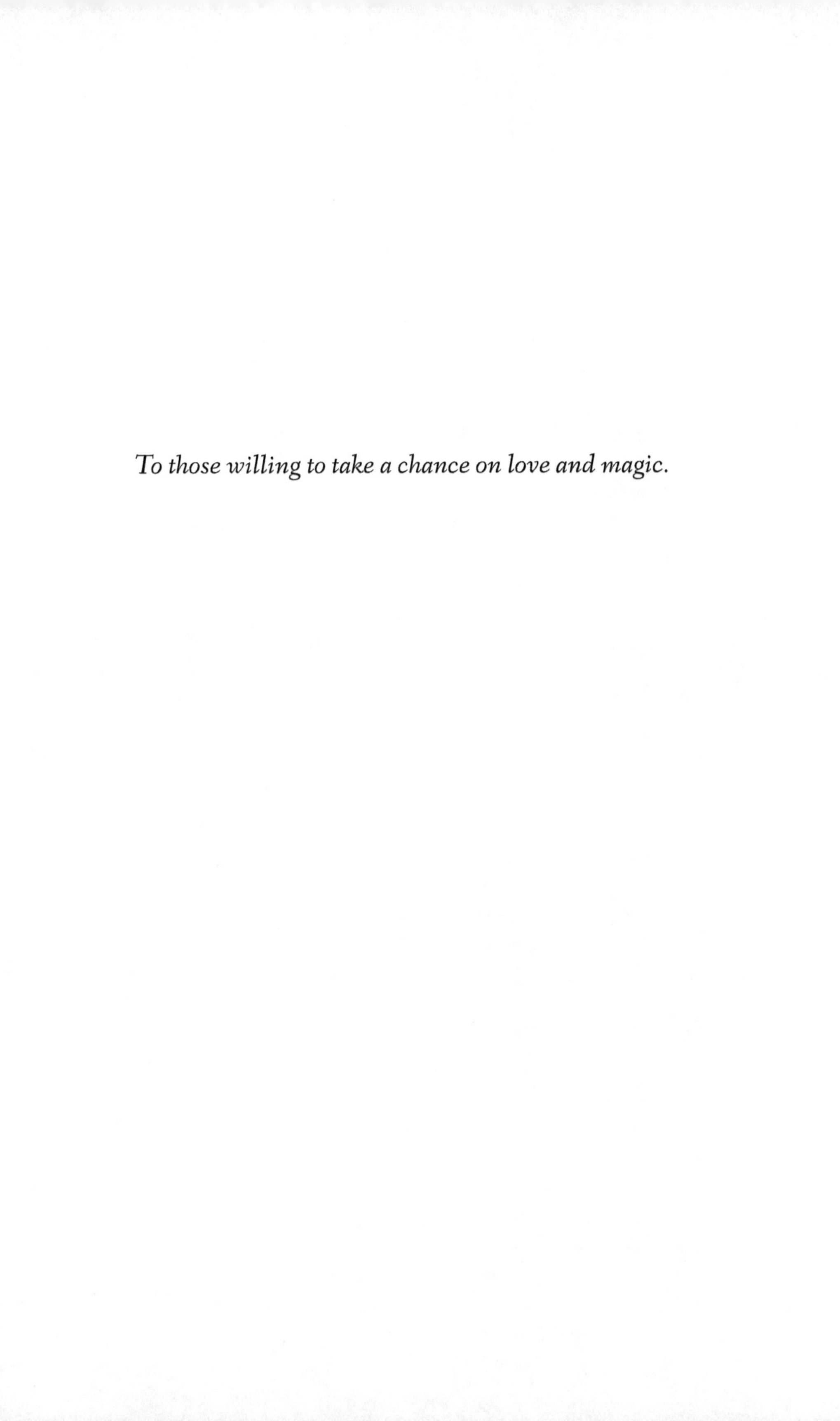

To those willing to take a chance on love and magic.

CHAPTER 1

"*H*ey, babe. I got a job with benefits."

Camille Delacroix rolled her eyes at the newest yahoo bellying up to the bar. He'd directed the comment toward the trio of tourists taking a break from sightseeing in her hometown of New Orleans, with all the grace and precision of an atom bomb.

When did things go from "What's your sign?" to "You wanna Snapchat?"

Worse still, the bottle-blonde to his left was actually buying that horrible excuse for a pick-up line. She tittered, batted her augmented eyelashes at the failed Shakespeare and, nodding with glee, she shimmied after him on her ankle-breaking heels, while her painted-on strapless dress defied gravity with each step.

"So, what kind of a name is Chance?"

Cam shifted her attention back to the bar, hoping to intercept the innocent questioner, and she spied the doe-eyed stare from a fresh-face cherub barely old enough to be sitting at the big kids' table. She dried her hands on the towel she kept slung over her shoulder, then winked at her regular patrons as they all answered in unison.

"His maman took one."

Raucous laughter rang out, and Cam grinned crookedly at the well-rehearsed, standard response. Tourists. She could almost hear the wheels spinning in the poor girl's head as she tried to make the connection. *Oh, to be so naïve.*

Chuckling, Cam took another sip of her watered-down whiskey sour and returned to work.

The normal Tuesday night crowd had gathered at Gator Bites; not so busy Cam felt like she needed to grow a third arm, but enough people to keep her entertained. Mardi Gras had come and gone months ago, and hurricane season wouldn't hit full swing for a while yet. She stared out at the patrons. What would it be like to live in the real world, unencumbered by the knowledge of what really was out there? Knowing you didn't truly belong....

"Oy, Cam. *Abita et trois rois etouffee,* ya?"

Cam smiled at the approaching waitress, and with a nod, she called back the order to the cook, then grabbed a beer from under the bar. She whistled some nameless tune from a half-forgotten dream, snapped off the beer's top, and set it down on Genevieve's tray.

"*Ça va, cher?*"

Genevieve's overly dramatic sigh told Cam her polite inquiry had opened a can of worms she probably didn't want to get involved in. Genevieve was a good kid; a little wet behind the ears, but her heart was in the right place. She oozed exaggerated tiredness, and a hint of something else.

Cam recalled eavesdropping on a conversation between her

and another waitress. She hadn't caught all of the details, but at least two male names had been mentioned.

One of the perks about being a bartender: she heard everything. Whether it was something told in confidence, a sought-after piece of advice, or whatever was overheard mixing drinks. Not much happened at Gator Bites that didn't pass by her radar. Granted, an extra set of senses tied to skills beyond the reach of most mortals didn't hurt either.

"Oh, Camille. You're so lucky you don't have pretty girl problems."

Camille arched her pierced right eyebrow up as the words tumbled out of the stately blonde's mouth. *Wow. Did everyone take their stupid pill this morning?*

The waitress had the decency to look embarrassed, though. Her perfectly porcelain cheeks turned an interesting shade of grayish pink, and her mouth formed a tiny "o" ringed by fire engine red lips.

"Oh, my God. No, I didn't mean it that way."

Yeah. 'Cuz there's a better way for that to sound. Camille leaned her elbow on the padded lip of the worn wooden bar, resting her chin in her palm, and waited for Genevieve to continue. A couple of the regulars craned their necks, leaning in closer to catch how she was going to dig herself out of this hole.

"Oh geez, Cam. I mean, you're beautiful, but it's in a different way."

Cam gave a deliberate, lazy blink, pondering the truth of the back-handed compliment. *Girl, you have no idea just how right you are.*

"Different" was how she'd managed to survive the past two hundred years living among mortal humans.

Skin dancer.

Her mother had told her those words when she'd asked why she could do things no one else could in their port town of Marseille. Years would pass before she truly understood the full ramifications of those two mismatched words.

Genevieve sputtered and fumbled, each apologetic excuse spiraling ever-downward. The patrons' laughs masked most of her coworker's words, and that was fine by her. Cam shook her head, patting the cherry-red waitress on the shoulder with a sympathetic grin.

"Order up!"

Saved by the bell.

Cam chuckled as Genevieve grabbed the piping hot dish from her hands so fast the scalding sauce nearly spilled on the pair of them.

"Excuse me, miss?"

She tossed the towel over her shoulder and prepared a smile for the voice to her right. "*Bonjour, cher.* Can I—"

Her tongue froze as an eerie pair of eyes too blue to be human regarded her with a cool interest.

Shit. He's fae. She could feel it in her bones. Skin dancers had the inherent ability to sense other magical beings. A piece of her mother's advice rushed to the forefront of her mind: "*Avoid revealing yourself to my people. Hiding in plain sight is simple and safe among the mortals, but do not trust those living beyond the Fade.*"

Not only was he fae, but he was also a damned powerful one to boot. She resisted the urge to rub away the prickling sensation creeping along her arms. Too bad, for the gesture would do nothing to extinguish the dangerous fire building just beneath her skin. Standing an easy six-and-a-half feet tall, dusty blond hair reaching to his shoulders, and a devastatingly sensual smile framed by a well-trimmed five o'clock shadow, he waited patiently for her to reengage her mouth.

"I mean, uh...." Now she was the one fumbling for the right thing to say. Karma was quick on the bayou. "Can I get you a drink?" She painted on her best flirtatious grin, shoving her momentary lapse deep into her mind as she waited for him to respond. Fingers crossed, she hoped he read her pause as attraction. Not too far from the truth, but her need to remain anonymous outweighed her need for some horizontal refreshment.

This time, luck was on her side. He turned up the heat, running his hand through his hair and pinning her with a smoldering grin. Her heart hammered beneath the thin white tank of her work uniform, though she refused to give in to his obviously practiced charms. Damn. The man wore handsome like a comfortable suit. Knowing his glamour masked his true face made her all the more curious to see him drop his guard.

Why was he here? The question tumbled around in her mind as she fell into his pools of impossible blue. His sharp ensemble of black jacket and silken ebony button-down shirt was a bit more formal than the rest of the crowd, but all kinds wandered through the doors of Gator Bites. Three-piece-suit businessmen and bikini-wearing tourists often stood shoulder to shoulder with the low-brow barflies, and no one judged. He could just be in for a drink. No need to panic. Not yet, at least.

"Tempting," he murmured, the seductive hint of a smile tugging at the corner of his full mouth. "But perhaps later. I was wondering if you could help me find an old friend." He held her gaze and placed a faded, yellowed square onto the bar. His long fingers lingered on the image before he passed it across the barrier. Cam steeled her resolve and reached for the picture. Although grateful for the forethought, she was still underprepared for the mirror's reflection looking back at her. Her blood iced over in her veins, but she had to keep up the charade.

It was her, a lifetime ago. Strawberry blonde hair coiffed in two perfect side rolls, bangs curled under, while long waves flowed over her shoulder. Thick, feathery lashes framed her brown eyes, and cherry red lipstick painted her lush mouth. Even though the sepia photo had lost most of its tones, in her memory, the colors still popped in dazzling array. Shreveport, Louisiana in the late 1940s had been full of life, and she'd lived it to its fullest. The war had ended, and prosperity had been in the air. She'd turned one of her family's businesses into a quaint restaurant and hotel for returning GIs. The young man in the photo with her was Dave. She'd never gotten his last name.

With a blink, she folded up her memories, then returned her gaze to the cyan eyes studying her every reaction. "Don't think I've seen anyone looking like that in here."

"Are you certain? Her name is Elizabeth Carver. I heard from reliable sources she lives in the area." He glanced around at the gathered patrons. "She would be much older now. Perhaps she has a daughter who stayed here?"

His lyrical accent pinned his point of origin somewhere far from the bayous, which kicked into gear the dormant butterflies in her gut. With a shake of her head, she passed the picture down to a couple of the older customers and, keeping one eye on the frowns and the other on the mysterious stranger, she played her role as the avid assistant.

Muttered negatives and unsureties filtered through the crowd, giving Cam time to further study the man. She caught the shimmer of his glamour, the natural shield of all fae creatures, which dialed down their ethereal appearance and allowed them to walk freely among the mortals. Others like him had to concentrate to keep up the illusion, but as a skin dancer, she simply changed her appearance. No mask required; her innate magic did all of the heavy lifting.

"*Chagren, cher.* Sorry," she said and retrieved the faded picture, adding what she hoped was a convincing grin as she returned it to him. "Maybe you have better luck at the next place, *oui?*"

"Thank you for your assistance..." He pinched the opposite corner of the yellowed paper, his eyes locking with hers, and electricity zinged through her body.

Trapped by his unnerving and unyielding stare, Cam dug her nails into her palm, refusing to fill in the lengthening pause with her name, until...

"Cam, can I get two Sazeracs and an order of fried oysters and hush puppies?"

The crowded bar sounds melted away, the world about her vanishing, until it was only her and him.

"*You will meet me outside in two minutes.*" His voice, tempting and alluring, brushed through the corners of her mind, and Cam clenched her jaw tight enough to nearly crack her molars. A captivating yet sinister smile curved his full lips as he added, "*Camille.*"

CHAPTER 2

Camille stared out into the crowd, rigid, as the mysterious fae sauntered toward the exit. His long strides never wavered from their course, yet every obstacle moved out of his path—waitresses, drunks, even the furniture seemed intent on getting the hell out of his way.

When the door had finally whooshed shut, Cam shivered, hoping to jolt the absent warmth back into her blood. She rubbed her hand along the leg of her jeans, desperate to banish the pins and needles tickling her palm.

Who the hell was he, and how the hell did he get into my head?

Cursing under her breath at social media and other technology, Cam spun scenario after scenario of escape, each one as ineffective as the next, while her watch told the grim truth: Time still ticked on, and not in her favor. Could she feign a migraine? Food poisoning? Sudden onset of death?

"Cam? You look distracted. Why don't you take a quick break?"

Her shoulders dropped, and she smiled halfheartedly at her manager's ordered suggestion. Big Rob patted her on the back, his shaggy head miles above her downturned face. He outweighed her by a Buick, and he was her boss, so "no" was not in the cards. Resigned, she tossed the towel onto the bar, then nodded up at the compassionate gray eyes.

"Uh, *merci, cher*. Back in a flash, *oui?*"

The burly man shook his head, a strangely warm grin splitting the ZZ Top-worthy beard. "Nah, *miouche*. Take your time. You never eat enough. Go on. Choo. Go outside and grab some fresh air."

Outside? Big Rob only called her "squirt" when he was in an overly jovial mood, which was rare, to say the least. She gnashed her teeth, angered by the obvious manipulation. She waved as pleasantly as she could, then ducked under her wooden shield. Tuesday was a jukebox night, the house band, Gilly's Gents, playing their other gig in Baton Rouge. Satchmo was blowing the blues like nobody's business, and she sought solace in the direction of the bathroom. Cowering behind the toilet was definitely not top on her list of ways to spend her break but going beyond the walls turned her blood to ice.

She'd always been so careful. How did this monster slip by her?

"I assure you, dear, I will be much more monstrous if you continue to keep me waiting."

A strange magnetic pull dragged her shuffling feet away from the safety of the ladies' room. "Get out of my head, bastard," she hissed between clenched teeth. Icy tendrils slithered across her bare arms as the tug on her spirit ventured into agony, and she flared her nostrils, forcing air past the constricting grip on her ribs.

He might be big and bad in the land of the fae, but this was her town.

After a handful of reluctant steps, she'd staggered through the kitchen to stand before the door leading into the alley. Her hand touched the doorknob and the electric crackle of magic beyond the barrier crept along her fingertips. Anger and compulsion blended into a powerful cocktail and she threw open the door. The metal bounced off of the red brick wall, and using the scant seconds before it swung shut, Cam stormed out into the awaiting dark.

ZACARIAS RESTED his elbow against the only clean spot on the cracked red-brick dividing wall. Thankfully, the restaurant's owners cared enough to keep their trash farther downwind, yet the mingling smell of the nearby swamp, the cloying magnolia blossoms, and general scent of humanity created an odor sure to linger on his skin long after leaving.

He sneered, folding his arms across his chest as two scantily dressed mortal females approached. They reeked of alcohol and arousal, the miasma cocooning the wobbling pair in a sickly chartreuse fog. One blonde rose up onto the balls of her stilettoed feet and batted her spidery eyelashes at him. The corner of his lip curled higher, and he shooed away the unwanted affections. Human minds were so easy to manipulate, and given their intoxicated state, he'd barely flexed his magic to send them on their way.

Again alone, Zacarias eyed the timepiece on his wrist as the gray metal door marked "Employees Only" flew open and a lone figure exploded onto the scene. His prey was taller than he'd expected, slender and fit. Nothing shimmered as she approached.

No aura wavered, and neither did her eyes shift in color from their haughty, rich green. He arched a brow, intrigued by her cocky visage.

So the rumors are true. The queen had indeed found a skin dancer: a being capable of magic so powerful, they could change their entire appearance; alter it on the deepest of levels, not merely mask any superficial aspects. Her approaching swagger bordered on cute, and if he hadn't already been irritated by her stalling, he might have been tempted to sample her plump lips.

He drank in her curves and her strength as she covered the distance between them with choppy steps, her close-fitting white top and low-slung pants putting her assets in a favorable light. Regrettably, any dalliances would have to wait until much later; matters of life and death hung in the balance, and he needed to keep a clear head. He tucked his inopportune desire into a steel cage in his mind, then dropped his chin and pinned her with a bored glare.

"You will find making me wait is not good for your continued anonymity."

The skin dancer he knew only as Camille stopped her determined strides and, holding his gaze, she crossed her arms low across her flat, exposed midsection, remaining on her side of the secluded alley. "Speak your piece. Ain't in no mood, *couillon.*"

Zacarias dragged in a sharp inhale. An insult? With a shake of his head, he kicked off the wall. "You will address me with proper respect." The air thrummed, and his little skin dancer narrowed her emerald green eyes. "I am Zacarias, Grand Enforcer of Tannequil, Queen of the Royal High Court of the Fae." He paused, anticipating the standard groveling.

It appeared Hell would become the next ski resort before she would bend a knee. She blinked up at him, the two slender silver hoops that pierced one graceful brow reflected the flickering gaslight overhead. Not even a flash of recognition had pinked her cheeks.

He frowned. "Do you know nothing of your history, child?"

Camille rested back into one shapely hip, and a deep crease wrinkled her smooth forehead. "Don't be callin' me 'child.' Got a whole full name, me."

"So I would assume. Care to share the information with the rest of the class?"

"Didn't know your kind went to school."

Unamused, he glared.

"Camille," she said. "Camille Anaïs Delacroix."

He cocked his head patiently, expecting her to complete her lineage, when in truth, he wanted to hear more of her unique voice. Rich and warm, it spoke of wildness and of vibrant life. Instead, she stared blankly at him. Rolling his eyes, he groaned in disappointment. "Is that all?"

An ear-blistering string of profanity in French flowed passed her full pink lips, and she stepped into his personal space, stabbing one finger into his chest. He gripped the digit tightly before it could strike again. Time was not in his favor, and his patience was waning with every second spent locked in his façade.

"Are you done?" Exasperation had laced his tired inquiry.

She struggled to wrench away her hand, irritation and indignation bleeding through her flowery perfume. *This is getting nowhere.* Clamping his jaw shut, he crowded into her, advanced as she retreated backwards until her ass hit the other side of the alley.

"Now. If you wish to remain peacefully hidden among the mortals, you will listen." Several emotions rippled across her aura, but she remained silent. "Her Majesty has requested your aide in a matter of some import," he said. "Your special abilities allow you to move undetected through the human population. Also, judging by your colorful vocabulary, you have become accustomed to their ways."

"Just you hang on—"

"I. Wasn't. Finished." He'd punctuated each word with a bite out of the scant space between them until her thinly veiled nipples were only a breath away from his chest. "An illness is affecting my people."

Her intriguing green eyes flashed, daring him to close the final distance, and she tipped her chin up, refusing to cower. "So call a doctor," she said, and he held her gaze, silently counting the passing seconds until realization had furrowed her brow. "Thought y'all couldn't get sick."

"We can't," he growled, tucking his tongue and his anger safely behind his teeth. "Neither plague nor common cold have affected my race, or any other fae race, in a millennium. Even those who pass between worlds have never succumbed to any human disease. Yet, in the last two months, two dozen of my brethren have died under mysterious circumstances and hundreds lay in sick beds. And now, Lysandra, daughter of my queen and heiress to the Lands Beyond the Fade, has fallen victim to this strange sickness."

His heart ached as he recalled the tears of Tannequil wracked by agonizing grief and helplessness as her youngest child wheezed and shivered beneath the thick furs. When the first body was found, panic and rumors had spread faster than the summer zephyrs. Illness had never touched his kind, yet with each passing dawn, more had been afflicted. He'd asked question after question, determined to discover the cause of these untimely and unnatural deaths. His duty as Grand Enforcer was to protect all of his people from enemies seen and unseen. Now, all he could do was sit, impotent, and watch his kin die.

"Like I said, call a doc. Not sure what good I can do for you."

He lowered his gaze to regard his companion. Still close enough to feel the heat from her inked skin, she stood her ground, arms folded beneath her pert breasts, while she stared at something in the center of his chest. He was tempted to reach up to ensure his glamour was still firmly in place.

"Humans may have been affected by this illness, as well. Have you heard of any strange deaths here?"

She slipped out of his reach and erupted in surprised laughter, head thrown back. Confused, he leaned away. Had he said something purposefully amusing?

"Dang, *cher*. This is New Orleans." Her smile tilted, the overhead light catching in her twinkling jade eyes. He knew the name of the city; a familiar hub for supernatural folk. Yet, this *N'Awlins* of which she spoke was new to him. "Folks turn up dead nearly once a day. Twice, if the weather's right."

Zacarias narrowed his eyes, and in one stride, he backed her against the red bricks. "These deaths would not appear as mere accidents or even acts of random violence."

Her crooked grin faltered, and he caught the hitch in her breath. Intrigued by the slip in her bravado, he maintained his close proximity, and her tongue flicked out, wetting her parted lips. "So, they'd look like what?"

"We do not know," he replied. A distant buzz tickled his thoughts like icy fingers. His queen was calling him, her sorrowful plea for news tugging on his spirit. *Damn.* "It could appear as a plague or viral spread of disease," he said. "I know little of humankind. It might even seem natural for mortals. Fever, convulsions, labored breathing have been seen in all victims. It moves at an alarming rate. However, from the exact time the first symptoms manifest until ultimate death is still unknown."

A curious frown creased her forehead, the delicate silver brow rings twinkling in the muted amber streetlights. "Wouldn't quick for y'all be instant for humans?" she asked.

"Not quite that fast. In truth, we have only seen one case at the beginning stages, and therefore, we do not know the initial warning signs." The itch inside his mind shifted to a searing pain. He must leave. Switching tactics, he stepped away from her, the distance cooling his blood. "I have no more time to waste here. Your queen has requested your assistance. Search for that which stands apart as odd. Another will be sent to guide you in your quest. I will return tomorrow, and I expect you to have made progress."

Her cheeks flushed. Indignation burned in her sparkling eyes, and he peered deep into the fiery green before him. Within, he spied strength, intelligence, and ... something else. Something more visceral than mere temptation. Pity that something would have to wait until later to investigate.

Zacarias lingered a moment longer, then he begrudgingly turned on his heels. He paused before opening the shadowed gateway, glancing over his shoulder.

"Fail in this, little one, and more than your secret will be lost." Certain his threat had hit its mark, he nodded, then stepped into the darkness.

CHAPTER 3

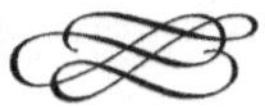

*A*lone in the alley once again, Camille blinked, rubbing her hands rapidly against her bare arms. Nearly two hundred years of peace and quiet had just disappeared, swallowed up by the inky dark behind the trash bin. Soon, laughter spilled in from the street, cementing her firmly in the present, and she considered her options, turning her face to the heavens. She prayed for the first time in years, her eyelids slipping shut as she asked for guidance, hoping someone upstairs was listening.

"Cam, *ça va, chère?*"

A familiar voice from the kitchen had cut into her one-way conversation with the powers that be. Was she all right? Only time would truly tell on that query.

Sighing heavily, she dropped her shoulders and, painting on a cordial smile, peered over to the slender Jamaican holding the back door open.

"Just takin' in the stars, Remi."

Remi frowned, the crease folding his ebony forehead nearly in half. "Ain't no stars about now, *chère*."

Cam didn't look up at the cloudy skies. Instead, she patted him on the shoulder, grinning as she squeezed past him. "Just 'cuz ya can't be seein' 'em, don't mean th'ain't there, *non?*"

His low mutterings rolled down her back, until a loud crash from the restaurant kicked her legs into gear. Combine the shattering with the tell-tale prickling of magic, and dread encouraged her to sprint the final distance. She dodged the incoming busboy, then skidded to a halt inside the main room.

She groaned, dropping her face momentarily into her palm, before raising her gaze to take in the mounting disaster. Patrons at several tables wiped drinks off of their sleeves, glaring at the stumbling newcomer.

What the hell? Is there a "Welcome Fae" sign I can't see above the door?

Tall, well-built, and clumsier than an ox, he bumped into another waitress while apologizing for his current mess. Luckily, Monica had safely delivered her drinks, though the contact had nearly knocked her into the table's occupants.

He swiveled about, grabbing onto Monica's arm. "Excuse me. I'm sorry."

A klutzy fae. He moved like a newborn foal on roller skates.

On black ice.

Blindfolded.

Cam gawked, mind racing while she drank in the catastrophic swath of destruction, and when the cause of the chaos turned to her, his face lit up. Swarthy skin glowed, and his soft brown eyes crinkled joyfully as he rushed over to her.

"It's you. It is truly you. Oh, thank the goddess. I found you."

He threw his arms around her in a bone-crunching bear hug, and she squeaked. Squirming, she managed to sneak her elbows between them, and she forced him away. He was dressed in an inconspicuous sleeveless white T-shirt and an out-of-style pair of faded blue jeans, both now decorated with splashes of hurricane pink. He beamed at her, and her brow furrowed. She would have remembered someone this clumsy.

"Cam? You know this guy?"

Eerie silence blanketed the bar as all eyes waited for her next words.

Think fast.

Now disentangled from the mysterious galoot, she stammered, scrambling for a believable explanation. She peeked up at her boss. "Uh, yeah? He's my, uh, cousin."

Big Rob narrowed his gaze, suspicion tugging up one corner of his mustache. "You sure 'bout that?"

Cam laughed nervously as she held the guy at arm's length, her grip tight on his biceps in case he wanted another grope. "It's, umm, just been a while since we've seen each other."

Her boss pinballed his gaze, bouncing between her face and that of her "cousin." Convinced, he nodded and headed back to his office down the hall. "A'ight. Just make sure he don't break no more inventory, *oui?*"

She bobbed her head, then shuffled him toward the bar. "*Merci.*" Blessed noise filled the void, and she shoved him toward the empty end of the bar.

Eighty years. Eighty years, she'd stayed out of the game, flying under the radar of every fae or shifter who happened by. She'd moved to new towns, had changed her job and her name so many times, she'd actually begun to keep a list so she wouldn't repeat herself. Hell, she'd even slept with an oblivious werewolf while visiting Toledo, Ohio in the early 1970s. Only now, after nearly two hundred years, she'd returned to her roots, making New Orleans her home and using her birth name. Pondering the cause of the increased magical activity would not solve this new wrinkle. She pinned the swarthy immortal with a serious stare.

"You better start talking," she said. "Who—"

"Cousin? Does that mean we are lovers?"

Her eyes nearly popped out of her head. "What?" Her stare darted around, and she prayed no one had heard his ridiculous question. "*Mon Dieu, non!* It means you're part of my family."

"Family." She watched his mouth move around the word, as if testing the flavor of each letter. A well-trimmed mustache and goatee framed full lips, and his pale brown eyes sparkled. When she blinked, his glamour slipped a fraction, revealing pointed features of glimmering gold. She shook her head and the illusion returned.

"Who are you?" Curiosity had blended with confusion as she held his gaze.

A broad grin split his face, and he placed a hand over his heart. "I am Rhys."

She blinked again, patiently waiting for him to continue, but he remained a smiling statue. "And ... ?" she encouraged.

"Aaaaaand"—his thick brows tugged together—"I'd like a beer?"

She tossed her hands toward the ceiling, desperate from some heavenly patience. "I figured out that much, Einstein," she grumbled. "Got more than a first name?"

He beamed, resting his closed fist over his heart. "Rhys

Valmary, Knight of the Fourth Order, loyal to the Lesser Court of the Fae."

Cam shifted her weight into her hip. "Knight?" While she found the guy mildly attractive, he was definitely not what she'd consider to be heroic material. Maybe fae society had a different meaning for the word.

"Yes. I was sent by the Lady Maeve, half-sister to the queen, to aide and protect you."

Her shoulders drooped. "Protect? From what?"

"From any dangers you may encounter as you quest," he replied, and he puffed out his chest, planting fisted hands onto his hips. Sadly, the pose reminded her more of Peter Pan than Superman. Maybe it was the outfit. Denims and white sneakers rounded out his collegiate ensemble. He must have gotten to the wardrobe after Zacarias had taken all of the cool clothes.

Help? She sighed tiredly and grabbed her damp bar towel from the counter. If this was help, she hated to think what a hindrance would look like. "I think you might be a few minutes late there, *cher.*"

Confusion wrinkled his brow. "Late? How can that be?"

Two fae in one evening. She ducked under the bar, needing the buffer of wood between her and her screwed up night. She'd lived for centuries, happily walking a fine line between the realms of humanity and magic. Now, in the space of thirty minutes, her entire world had been turned upside down.

Movement to her left caught her attention, and she raised a hand, stopping her would-be champion from joining her behind the barrier. She snagged a couple beers from the fridge, sorting through her thoughts. The physical repetitive task of fixing drinks often gave her a chance to process offers and options.

"Already met Zacarias," she said.

The color from Rhys's cheeks drained. "The Grand Enforcer?" he stammered, his gaze darting into every darkened corner. "He is here?" He knocked his knees against the bottom of the railing, jumping to his feet.

Cam groaned, shaking her head. "He's long gone. Left out the back way just 'fore you come in." With an inquisitive gaze, she locked eyes with Rhys. "Now, how long have you been here?"

"Here?" Rhys cocked his head, reminding her of her neighbor's poodle. "Why, I had only arrived moments before you found me and—"

She waved off the rest of his rambling. "*Non, cher,*" she said. "I mean how long 'here.'" She pinched his forearm, hoping he understood her unvoiced query. In her gut, she knew the answer, but she'd asked anyway.

His brown eyes sparkled, and again he beamed in pride. "This is my first venture into the ... the city."

She released the breath she'd been holding, grateful for his self-correction. Fabulous. Just what she needed: a powerful fae holding the keys to her past, and a sidekick stumbling around in a new skin suit. Her head thumped onto the thick, padded bumper, and she hid in the welcoming dark.

Strains of "Dream a Little Dream" filled the room. *Finally.*

She raised her head, plastering on her standard end-of-the-night expression. "Y'all know the drill. You don't gotta go home..."

"But you can't stay here," replied the gathered patrons in smiling unison. She must have missed last call while she was on break. A shudder danced along her spine at the memories of her earlier encounter. Sensuality clung to Zacarias like a spider's web —delicate, yet inescapable. Her skin still tingled from his brief contact, and if she were honest with herself, she hungered for more. Farewells rang out, tips lined the bar and, back in the moment, she waved her thanks as the room emptied.

As she wiped down the wood, Rhys's gaze followed her every move, his intense analysis only slightly unnerving. What concerned her more was the dilemma of his housing. Her current abode, a small one-bedroom above the bar, would make for cramped quarters at best. She could secret him out to one of her old family's estates in Thibodaux, but that would mean transportation. Her car was in a lot not too far away, but she was hesitant to get onto the roads after the bars had stopped serving. Sighing, she paused, her closing duties now finished, and she shifted her gaze to her studious observer.

What am I going to do with you?

As she ducked under the bar, she continued to contemplate possible places to stash him.

"So," he said, "are we to have sex now?"

She lunged toward him and slammed her hands over his mouth. "*Ta gueule!* No." A frantic survey of the deserted bar encouraged her heart to return to its regular pace, and she huffed out the remaining air in her lungs. "Why ... what ... who even says that?"

The confused puppy look returned as muffled words filtered through her fingers. She dropped her shoulders, met his narrowed eyes and, taking a chance, removed her hands.

"Is that not what humans do at the end of each day?"

This was going to be a long night.

CHAPTER 4

Camille took another sip, hoping the next swallow of tepid coffee would spark a solution. Tomorrow, she could ship her houseguest deep into the bayous and hopefully out of her hair for good. Until then, she was stuck with him.

She regarded him coolly, drained by his exhausting curiosity as he surveyed every inch of her tiny apartment. Rhys marveled at her meager collection of trinkets; he picked up each item and twisted it this way and that, before setting it back, slightly askew. Under his breath, he remarked on its texture or inquired about its use, and her patience waned the longer the game of "what does this do" dragged on. Kleenex fascinated him, and once he had nearly decimated her last box, she took to her feet.

"Okay, okay." She grabbed away the flimsy cardboard box as the last square of tissue fluttered to the ground. "You know, you're gonna have to pay for all those." She discarded the empty container into the trash can in the kitchen, adding it to the growing pile of broken knickknacks. A bottle opener, two lamps, and a sock monkey lay in pieces over coffee grounds and banana peels. She shook her head and dug deep to find her composure. Once in control of her temper again, she shifted her gaze to her bumbling knight.

Knight. She scoffed at the word. If this was the fae's idea of chivalry, she was grateful to be living among the humans. So far, he'd saved her from the answering machine, slayed a handful of junk mail, and scared the crap out of her cat. Alley would come back as soon as she was hungry; hopefully her fur would be its normal color when she did. Cam pinched the bridge of her nose, focusing on the pinpoints of pressure and ignoring the surrounding chaos.

She had survived the Reign of Terror, the American Revolution, and every other conflict since. How hard would it be to last a few hours with an overly curious fae?

A delicate crash split the growing silence. Clamping down on her molars, she peeled her eyelids open. At least Rhys had looked sheepish as he scrambled to pick up the slender glass slivers. The image itself had no sentimental value, so no giant loss; she'd only bought it because she liked the frame and she needed to have some kind of family pictures decorating her place, even if the family wasn't hers.

"All right, that's enough." She stormed over to Rhys, whose gaze darted around her tiny apartment, most likely searching for a place to hide from her anger. He feigned left, but she read his obvious ploy and grabbed on to his shoulders, then shoved him backwards until he plopped onto the couch. She huffed in short breaths as she gathered her thoughts. "Sit your ass down and try not to destroy everything I own."

Her finger doubled as a weapon, aimed directly at his chest, as she hovered above him. "You show up in my bar, spouting some crap about being sent to help me out. Help, how? By screwing up my life so much, I have to do whatever it is you ... you people want me to do?"

"You are upset?" Rhys had whispered the simple question, his dawning realization having dialed down the volume of his voice. Wide eyes blinked at her, while confusion and curiosity rippled across his shimmering mask.

Was he innocent? Was he merely a pawn, like her? She struggled to rein in her emotions, to allow her rational mind to analyze the facts.

Fact number one: Eighty years of anonymity had apparently been blown in the course of a couple of hours.

Fact number two: The Court of the Fae knew much more about her than she knew about them.

Fact number three: Her fate was now in the hands of two fae, one of which seemed solely bent on getting her into the sack.

She locked her jaw, refusing to look away from her guest. "Rhys?"

A coy smile tugged up the corner of his lips. "Yes?"

"Do you like your hands attached to the ends of your arms?"

He nodded slowly, his lids drifting down. "I very much do."

"Then you'd better get them off my ass, or you're gonna be picking them up off the floor."

His face froze, eyes as wide as saucers. *Good.* While her prey was dumbfounded, she scooted back, slipping out of his unwelcome embrace, and once again at a safe distance, her thoughts returned to the main problem. Looked like she was going to be stuck with immortal help, whether she wanted it or not, until she finished her task.

So how was she supposed to find information about a sickness affecting the fae world? Hell, she was no doctor. She flipped through her memories and didn't even find one medical person in her list of her other selves. Fear had kept her away from professions requiring serious knowledge. Doctors and lawyers made decisions that could alter people's lives. Plus, she wasn't a fan of the sight of blood.

She tugged at her lower lip and stared out the window. The amber gaslights twinkled along St. Ann Street, warming the base of the inky black sky, while the thumbnail moon played hide and seek with her between the broken clouds. The night was so peaceful, so tranquil. She wondered what it would be like to live—to fully live—in the world around her. Family, children, a stable home, surrounded by people who loved her. Someplace where she didn't have to hide who and what she was. Her mother had found happiness. Why couldn't she?

Images beyond the glass blurred, and she blinked rapidly, dismissing the threat of surprised tears. What was with the pity party? Probably exhaustion, coupled with the influx of unwanted attentions. Dashing a hand across her leaking eyes, she paused, feeling the weight of another's gaze following her movements. An awkward silence had blanketed the room. She arched an eyebrow and glanced over her shoulder.

He hadn't moved. Not an inch. Mouth still slightly agape, Rhys held his rigid pose, arms extended, embracing his invisible partner. Only the occasional blink proved he wasn't a statue.

Let him stay like that. She shooed away the little voice in her mind and heaved an exasperated sigh.

"Relax," she said, "I'm not going to bite." She headed into the kitchen to grab something else to drink, tossing an additional suggestion back into her living room, "And you can drop the glamour in here. No one else is gonna be coming to join us. Just be yourself."

"Will you?"

The odd question halted her refrigerator rummaging, and she peered over the top of the white door. "Huh?"

Rhys stood in the center of her apartment, still cloaked in his disguise. He stuffed his hands into his pockets. "Will you do the same?"

She blinked slowly. Will she do what? Relax? A light flicked on in the back of her head. "Do you mean, am I going to drop my glamour?"

"I ... I wouldn't want to be comfortable while you were not." He dipped his chin sheepishly.

Huh. Maybe he is a knight after all. Touched by his chivalrous gesture, she grinned crookedly as she fished out two bottles of Coke. "Not the same. I don't have to hide who I am. Well, not in the way you do."

With a sharp nod, he shifted, shivering from head to toe, and Cam watched in stunned silence as the glamour crumbled to the ground like confetti tossed from balconies during Mardi Gras. The slivers of ethereal gold disappeared into her worn beige carpet, leaving no trace. She hip-checked the fridge closed and headed back to her guest.

By their nature, fae creatures were devastatingly beautiful; features honed by magic and the power of the elements so compelling they sent mortals into a sexual frenzy. Cam often wondered if her parents had met that way, but quickly dismissed her silly thought. Her father had never seemed controlled by her mother. If anything, it was Mom who'd been smitten with Dad. Her mixed blood worked as a protective shield against the pull of her distant lustful relations.

In her long past, Cam had spent a night or twelve tangled in the sheets with a handsome partner, but always on her own terms and never with the aid of magical influences. Yet the longer she stood in Rhys's presence, the more she realized he might not need any otherworldly assistance either. He was tall and attractive, with a swarthy complexion that glowed with inhuman radiance. Eyes of swirling topaz blinked at her, and his ebony curls remained tidy. Still the same man who'd nearly squeezed the stuffing out of her in the bar, only somehow more. She attributed her current immunity to the weight of her unwanted task and her improvised familial connection.

"Feel better?" She handed him an open bottle, then sank down into her usual place on the couch. She kicked her feet up onto the coffee table and started to unlace her combats, the mundane activity centering her mind on her newly acquired royal duties. Zacarias would pop back in on her sometime tomorrow, and she had no idea how to find what it was he wanted.

What did he expect her to do? Sneak into the hospitals and morgues? Eavesdrop on the police for details? She did own a computer, so maybe a search of local news reports would be enough to keep him happy. Once her toes were free from their steel-and-leather cages, she returned her gaze to her strange houseguest.

He held the glass bottle cautiously, uncertainty pulling the corners of his goatee down into an adorable frown. "And this is...?"

"It's harmless," she answered, chuckling, and she took a long swallow from her own drink in demonstration. "Just sugar, water, and a laundry list of unpronounceable ingredients."

He sniffed tentatively, wrinkling his nose at the bubbly onslaught. He took a careful sip, then grinned, apparently pleased with the results, and nearly decimated the contents in one gulp. A bigger, more satisfied grin warmed his face for only a moment, soon replaced by an inquisitive visage.

"Is this your normal face?"

She groaned, slinking down into the battered sofa. "Why are you so fascinated by this? Yes. This is my normal face. This is just who I am."

"And your ... your voice? Your speech patterns?" He moved closer, perched on the edge of the low table. "They have changed since we entered your home. The regional affectations have audibly diminished."

Ah, the little details. Yawning, Cam stretched her arms over her head, careful not to allow her tank top to reveal too much skin, her eyes drifting shut. "Gotta keep up the character at work. When I was hired, that's how I talked."

"But, doesn't it drain you?"

Not as much as this conversation does. Cam peeled open her heavy lids and, keeping her comments to herself, leveled her tired gaze at him. "Not in the way you're thinking. I don't think too much on it." He hung on her every word, looking eager for more, and a pitiful whine slipped past her lips. "You're not going to let this go, are you?"

Light twinkled in the depths of his unique eyes. "To be in the presence of a living skin dancer? Our histories have little to no information on the nature of your magicks. Nor has there been anyone aside from the immediate royal family who has spent time with one of your line."

"Yeah, well. Whoop-dee-friggin'-do," she grumbled under her breath. "Glad I'm such a hot commodity. Right now, though, I've got a question or two myself. First off, why me, and why you?"

His lack of response caught her attention. He batted his long lashes, and she stared, hypnotized by the rapid fluttering. "I don't quite understand either of your queries," he replied.

Cam chuckled sleepily. "Well, I guess that makes two of us. That really didn't make much sense. I mean, can't your people just do your own looking here? What can I do that makes me so ... so special? And just what short straw did you draw to get landed with babysitting duties?"

Rhys slid gracefully off her coffee table and knelt at her feet. "Camille," he breathed in awe, "you can do things my people can only imagine. You can alter your very skeletal structure and become a completely new individual. We fae can only mask our appearance, and for rather limited amounts of time. As for me, I... I volunteered for the opportunity to help."

The level of near-idolatry in his voice chilled her blood, but it was the well-timed hesitation that piqued her interest. She recalled her mother's warning of her distant kins' natures, and their volatile opinions of her uniqueness. "*I was a rare child and unwelcome by many within the High Court of the Fae. You, ma chère, have inherited both my gifts and your father's human kindness and generosity. This will make you a target should any of my kind discover you. Do not trust them. Not even if the faces they wear appear fair.*"

And his face was rather fair. Without the aid of his glamour, his pale brown eyes glowed with flashes of golden lightning. Not to mention, his height did give him an advantage. She shook her head rapidly, banishing her curious id and rattling her logical self to the forefront. "There has to be more to it than that," she said, before pointing an accusatory finger his direction. "And don't think I didn't catch that pause. Look, it's late," she continued, her arm dropping heavily into her lap. "I'm really tired, and I have no way of knowing how to solve a mystery involving an illness that affects faes but maybe not humans."

Once she'd spoken the words aloud, the weight of her task dragged her spirit straight through the floor. *This is crazy. What the hell does that asshole expect me to do?*

"That asshole expects you to fulfill your duty."

The rich, sensual, and very unexpected voice tumbled through her foggy thoughts. "Are you friggin' kidding me?"

"Beg your pardon?"

Cam waved off Rhys's polite inquiry and climbed to her feet. "Not you. HIM." She flailed her arms toward everything and nothing.

"Who, him?"

The perfect, synchronous harmony of Zacarias's voice in her head and Rhys's confused tone would have been funny, had she not been exhausted beyond belief. She spun about, pinning the only male present with a ball-shriveling stare. "You know, I'm not playing this game tonight."

Although her patience was being sucked further into the floor, her deeply ingrained Southern hospitality held tight. Cam stomped over to the tiny linen cabinet and snatched out the spare pillow and a blanket, even as she grumbled. Too much upheaval; she needed time to decompress.

After adding a towel to the stack of linens, she tossed the entire pile in Rhys's general direction. "Enjoy the couch," she declared. "I am going to bed in my own room, AND NO BOYS ARE ALLOWED."

She slammed the frail door, the needed exclamation mark clear and final.

CHAPTER 5

Sleep refused to give Camille a respite for more than a few moments. Inside her head, the arguing voices rose and fell like waves on a distant shore. At least all of the speakers were of her own making; the two males who had recently invaded her life were surprisingly silent. Her mother had warned her of the dangers of getting involved with the fae court. *"Do not trust them, ma chère. Though they may be beautiful to the eyes, their hearts are filled with vipers. They care naught for others. Keep them at an arm's length, always."* Before they'd fled to the New World, she'd send Cam to bed each night with grim stories of the fairy folk. Now, tales of manipulative cruelty and selfish devotion echoed through her memories and guided many of her daily adult decisions.

"Knowing an enemy is close at hand is the best way to keep one step ahead of trouble." Her father had joined in, his deep voice blending in loving harmony with his cautionary words. Years had passed since she'd last heard her parents' voices, but she'd never

"

forget the soothing comfort that would blanket her troubled thoughts whenever she recalled the melodic timbre. Their deep love had shone in their eyes and made all of her worries float away like wishes made on dandelion heads. In all her lonely years, whenever she was filled with doubt or fear, she'd imagine the sage wisdom and encouraging words from them.

"What do I do, *maman?*" she whispered as she continued to contemplate the ceiling, transfixed by the lazy circles of the cooling fan. But soon, the breaking dawn crept across the popcorned surface, ushering in a new day. Cam grumbled and kicked off the covers to crawl out of her confining bed. The sooner she attacked the problem, the sooner she would be rid of her other-worldly interlopers.

She rubbed the sleep out of her eyes and planted her socked feet onto the floor. Coffee. This day would need buckets of coffee. She glanced down at her attire and contemplated her borderline nakedness. Given the company beyond the door, she'd decided to rummage through her underwear stash before curling up under the sheets. The matching tank and short pairing she'd chosen had been more of a joke from her burly boss than a serious sleeping outfit. She hated pink, so of course the bright fuchsia booty shorts and corresponding-colored letters boldly declaring, "Professional Bitch. Don't try this at home," stamped across the ribbed white fabric had stayed buried in the top dresser drawer. *On second thought....* She grabbed the tattered sweater off the back of the chair and yanked on the faded charcoal wool cardigan, then opened her bedroom door.

She half-expected to see Rhys either passed out on her couch or still standing in frozen vigil after her less-than-graceful exit from the previous night. Neither met her eye, and she blinked to verify her current view.

"You cleaned my apartment."

Not that she was a slob, of course. She simply believed a house should look as if people actually lived there. Granted, when she was working double shifts, her place might have given a couple of the frat houses at LSU a run for their money, but it was never so bad that anyone had complained. Yet, as she scanned the scene beyond her bedroom door, she had a difficult time believing she hadn't heard him work. The floor was immaculate, the wood sparkling in the early rays of unfiltered sunlight. Pictures hung perfectly level in their scattered arrangements, and the few knickknacks on her shelves looked bare without their gray dust coats.

Rhys popped his head over the kitchen counter, a proud smile splitting his face. "Oh. Good morning. Did you sleep well?" He rose to his feet, revealing a bare chest and the distinct possibility of a similar view awaiting below the worn marble surface. *And I was worried about showing a little ass cheek.*

"Sorta. Rhys, why are you cleaning my house?" She carefully padded across the icy-slick surface and skated into the kitchen. "And where the hell is my coffee cup?" Steeling her nerves for whatever might meet her on the other side of the bar, she breathed out a sigh of relief when she spied pants. Low slung and hanging on to his narrow hips for dear life, but at least his goods were covered.

"I hope you don't mind. I thought I would make you some breakfast as a way to thank you for your hospitality, but then I noticed the dishes in the sink. I washed them but realized I didn't know where they should be placed. I rearranged your cupboards, organized your cutlery based on need and usage. And then I..."

She ignored his prattling as she poured herself a cold cup from the remains of yesterday's pot. The sharp bitterness kicked her groggy mind into gear, adding needed clarity to the strange morning. Fresh go-juice would have been better, but she was never one to waste. So, grateful her microwave was still attached above the stove, she popped the mug in for a warm-up, when her patience hit its limit and she spun around to face her blabbering guest.

"Okay, stop." Cam lifted her hand, hoping the universal "shut up" sign also worked on immortals. Too much needed to get done and listening to the whys and wherefores of Rhys's housekeeping regimen was not helping. "You did me a solid. Thank you. Now I need to get a game plan going for today."

"Game plan?" Rhys set the rag down onto the immaculate marble, eyeing her with hungry intent. "Are we going to have sex now?"

As she stood toe to toe with the full sensual force of the knight of the fae realm, she responded the only sensible way possible. She folded her arms across her chest and stared blandly at him. "Rhys," she said, "if I didn't jump into the sack with you last night, what ever makes you think today will be any different?"

A boyish twinkle danced in his topaz eyes. "Can I not stay hopeful?"

She shook her head in amusement, laughing lightly. "You'd have better luck hoping for winning lottery numbers. Right now, I've gotta get this whole mess straightened out so I can get back to my own life."

A soft ding behind her kicked her body into action. She

retrieved her lukewarm coffee, then slammed down the half cup, before grabbing her cell phone off the charger. Fingers crossed, she dialed the bar as she wandered toward her bedroom. While counting the number of rings, she snatched the jeans spilling out the drawer, added a pair of undies and a fresh T-shirt to the pile, and stepped into the bathroom.

"C'mon, Rob," she muttered, dropping the armload of clothes onto the white wicker hamper. "Pick up, pick up." Years of multi-tasking had honed strange skills for Cam, and one of the best was the ability to get dressed while brushing her teeth. She'd scarcely squeezed the white paste onto the narrow brush head, when a familiar voice answered from downstairs.

"Gator Bites. Your dime."

"*Bon matin*, Rob." Her heavy accent had returned in earnest as she once again stepped into her current role. "Oy, *cher*. Mind if I—"

"Please tell me y'ain't gonna be bringin' that cousin of yours by today? That boy's a walking accident ready to happen, and I don't wanna be refundin' no more money." Even though her boss's tone was jovial, she sensed the steel in his words. *This might be easier than I thought.*

"*Chagren.* But he's gonna be stayin' for a day or two, and he wants me to show him the city and—"

"Hey, that's a great idea!" Big Rob barged in again. "Why don't you take a couple days and keep him occupied? Never take no time off for yourself, you do. Would do you some good to get out." At this, Cam bounced in a silent happy dance before returning to her conversation.

"*Ta sûr?* You sure? Mean, don't want y'all to be stuck."

"*Non, non, miouche.*" She must have caught him at a good time, since he was still calling her "squirt." Things were looking up. "'Sides, Erik's been buggin' me for more shifts. Needs to learn more 'bout the place, he do. Now, shoo. Don't let me be seein' y'all 'til that cousin of yours is back home, *oui?*"

"*Merci, cher. À bientôt.*"

Cam ended the call and breathed a grateful sigh of relief. With her job safe for the time being, she rushed through her morning routine to take on her task. Zacarias had said to look for what was out of place. The Big Easy wasn't known for its mysterious death tolls. Most of the bodies that washed up along the riverbanks or were discovered in back alleys had obvious signs of violent struggles. Some were self-inflicted, be it drugs, alcohol, or a toxic combination of both. She couldn't recall the last time an "unusual circumstance" corpse had made the news.

"Time to fire up the laptop."

IN ALL THE thousands of years Rhys had walked the Land of Youth Beyond the Fade, never had he been rebuked ... furthermore by a creature of such power and beauty. He stared at the door left slightly ajar at her passing, fascinated by the flickering shadows of her criss-crossing path in the chamber beyond. Perhaps her mixed heritage had provided a level of resistance his brethren had failed to notate. An immortal skin dancer mother and a human father. What were the odds their offspring would have inherited the best of both worlds?

She spoke in a direct manner similar to all humans he'd encountered in this, his initial visit to the mortal realm. She also possessed the innate magicks whispered of only in rumor. It did not cause her aura to shine; it was almost unconscious to her. He could neither smell nor sense it along his skin. She was simply ... unique.

She was also quite confusing. She'd opened her home to him. Wasn't that a sign intimate relations would be occurring?

He would think more on her odd responses later. When she'd rejoined him in the larger room, her lean body was again wrapped in the clingy, pale blue fabric and a loose-fitting orchid tunic with sleeves reaching nearly past her fingertips. Tucked beneath her arm was a strange, slender silver box, and her socked feet padded silently across the blonde wood floor. An unfamiliar tune filled the air as she hummed, crossing to the small table. Her appearance was identical to their initial meeting—hair blacker than night spilled down her back, the thick raven curtain shimmering in the streaming sunlight. He pondered at the colorful images that had adorned her arms, curious if the ornate designs had vanished overnight.

"Would you stop staring at me?" A lingering trace of her exotic accent swirled around her words; hints of proper French danced with something he could not define. If he heard more, though, perhaps he could place it. Her eyes remained focused on the now unfolded box and the shimmering image before her. She tapped her fingertips across its base, striking small squares with precise intent.

He crossed to her seat for a closer inspection, hovering over her shoulder. Pictures and words appeared on the face of the box, detailing an increase in flu-like illnesses plaguing children of a place called the South Seventh Ward.

"What kind of magic is this?" Awestruck, he leaned in to study the odd contraption and its window peering into nothingness.

"It's not magic, *cher*. It's called technology." She had yet to regard him with her gaze, her brow furrowed in deep concentration. "Specifically, a laptop computer with a halfway decent processor when it's got a strong internet connection. This," she said, her hand gesturing toward the now-static image even as she slid her feet into the same blood-red boots she had worn the previous night, "is how we find out where to start looking for clues."

"Technology." He tasted the word, sampling it on his tongue. "I have heard tell of such science in my realm. It is said to have eyes that can see across the world, and any manner of information and entertainments can be found with its use."

She paused, her delicate fingers halting in their task of securing the boots' long laces. "Yeah, it's pretty amazing. Now, if you would back off and stop breathing down my neck, I could get this done a lot faster."

"Does my nearness draw you away from your task?" Her bowed back was nearly flush against his bare chest, her tresses like silk on his skin.

Her breathy sigh appeared to be laced more with exasperation than exhilaration. "If you're that horny," she said, "just knock on the door across the way. I think Janice is in a lull and would love the attention."

Another refusal?

Rhys rose to his full height. "Yet, you are uninterested?"

She groaned once again, dropping her tense shoulders before turning to face him. "Rhys, you seem decent enough, but I choose who I take into my bed. And right now, with Zacarias's edict hanging over my head, I'm not really in the mood, if you get my drift."

He peered into her eyes—the pools of pure, sparkling jade betrayed no guile. She simply was not interested in sexual relations at this time. Perhaps later she'd be more amiable to a friendly night of passion. She did have a point, however. The task she'd been given was daunting and all of their combined faculties would be needed to save his people. And should he fail in his part, his life might as well be forfeit.

"Prove yourself worthy or be cast out, Knight Valmary." The parting words of his queen stole away his desire for intimacy, chilling his immortal blood.

Nodding sagely, he eased out of her personal space, though remained within arm's reach. He opted to initiate conversation to break the tension.

"I do understand. Have you discovered something?"

Her slender brows tugged together as if weighing his sudden segue. "Uhh, yeah." She swiveled back about, squaring her shoulders to the laptop device, her head trailing behind. She gave him one final backward glance before returning to the flickering image. "There's a report of a high number of kids coming down with something like a flu in the South Seventh. The flu is generally a problem during winter, so it does bear checking into."

"Is it far from here?" he asked woefully. Rhys enjoyed moving around unencumbered by the energies expended on his glamour. Outside, the constraints would again be in place. More questions spun around his mind. Did she ever feel the drain on her magicks, keeping up her façade for as long as she did? He filed away the inquiry for later examination.

She shook her head and took to her feet, sliding the chair

against the slick floor. "*Non.* S'about a ten-minute streetcar ride, then another ten-minute walk to St. Mary's Hospital."

"Hospital?" He shuffled back to avoid the moving obstacle and to keep pace with her. "Are you ill?"

She scoffed, reaching for the messenger bag slung over the couch. "Me? Nah. But if there is some information, that would be the first place to see what they know." She strode toward the entrance, then stopped, fingers hovering above the rounded knob. "You coming or what? But"—she raised her hand, severing any comment from him—"you might want to change into something less ... well, less you."

"Less me?" He cocked his head, contemplating her strange request.

She pinched the bridge of her nose, then gestured in his general direction. "Yes. Clothes would be a good start. Humans normally wear them. And tone down the glow, would ya?"

Ah, yes. He glanced down at his current condition, and an impish thought crossed his mind, tugging up the corners of his lips. Perhaps he did have an effect on her after all.

"Okay, stop with the leery eye. Y'ain't gonna be blending in out there looking like you do now." She ducked under the bag's strap, freeing her hair from its momentary trap. "And no. I can read your thoughts from here. I'm still not going to jump into the sack with you."

Was telepathy one of her talents? "The Elders said nothing of that ability." Lest he offend her further, he inhaled deeply and, finding the source of his magic, he called to mind the image of his persona from the previous night. He slipped into the guise, securing the ethereal garment to his aura, then opened his eyes and met her gaze. Her slight smile was all the approval he desired. For now.

"*Bon*," she said, nodding sharply. "Now, I have a trick or two up my sleeve," she replied as she grabbed a small ring of keys from the table beside the door and waited for him to exit. "But that one? Yeah, I was exaggerating."

CHAPTER 6

Camille felt a twinge of guilt for fibbing to Rhys, but it was so obvious what he'd been thinking. Hell, he was practically licking her with his eyes. She had given him a decent lead if he really wanted to get laid; all Janice had done for the past week was mope around and whine about her sex life, which only made Cam question more her own staunch refusal of Rhys's offer for a roll in the hay.

Glancing over her shoulder, she appraised her assistant. He was attractive; she'd give him that. Tall, dark, and handsome. The "tall" was definitely a must in her book. She could be any height, but if she was going to take a man into her bed, he'd better reach from post to post.

But more importantly, he wasn't Zacarias.

Did he really have to be?

She had called Rhys her cousin as an emergency measure. In the light of day, she realized just how close to the truth her familial moniker had been. The distance between their lines, though, spanned chasms and worlds. If she did get together with him, it wouldn't be like kissing her brother. And he did have an endearing charm. None of the guys she'd ever dated had taken the time to pick up their underwear, much less clean her entire apartment.

Once again, the angel on her shoulder tapped its foot, perturbed by her fickle conscience, and she pinched her hand, the slight sting centering her wandering mind. No way would she ever truly have a forever relationship with either of them. Rhys was not her normal fare, and Zacarias had made it quite clear she was nothing more than a tool, a gofer to find something for a monarch she neither knew nor cared to know. Her mother had warned her about getting involved with any of the fae realm, and now here she was, an unwilling minion to the fae queen herself.

"Torn between a knight and a grand enforcer for my troubles," she muttered as they boarded the Rampart-St. Claude line streetcar heading toward South Seventh Ward. Certain her shadow was only a step behind, she hung on to the handrail and watched the city flow past the open window. Last night's rain had washed away the lingering backwater stench from the heat, leaving the light fragrance of magnolias in the air. The day was still early, though the clouds overhead threatened a deluge any second. For now, she took a deep, cleansing breath and refocused on today's trouble.

The streetcar bounced in its comforting pace, the swaying rhythm peaceful and melodic. Calm ... until she was nearly knocked off of her feet by a walking accident.

"Excuse me. Pardon me."

She rolled her eyes as pained interjections blended with

muttered apologies. What short straw had she grabbed to get such a clumsy sidekick? *At this rate, I'm gonna end up going into hock to keep the shirt on my back.* She glanced up at the map above the windows. Three more stops. How much damage could he do in three more stops?

A splash of cold liquid ran down the back of her leg, a sticky response to her unvoiced query.

"I'm so sorry there, sweetie." The kindly voice had centered around her waist, and Cam turned to find a flustered older lady digging into her purse. Assuming she was searching for some Kleenex or napkins to dry off the spilled whatever-it-was, Cam shook her head and patted the woman on the shoulder.

"S'all good, *chère*. Gonna help keep me cool today, *non?*" Cam grinned, then she crowded Rhys into the farthest and safest corner of the car. She grabbed his collar and yanked his face down to her level. "Would you please try to not cause a riot wherever you go?"

"How is it you can move about so freely within these—"

She slammed her palm across his mouth before anything truly crazy spilled out, balancing with practiced grace on the balls of her feet in her combats. "Don't even think about finishing that thought out loud." She locked eyes with his flared topaz orbs and held his gaze, until a resigned sigh slipped between her fingers. Her forehead ached from her constant eyebrow exercises, and she cast a sidelong glance over her shoulder. The car was comfortably full, with a mixed blend of locals and tourists enjoying the rhythmic bounce and sway. Thankfully, most of the riders were lost in their own realities, either rocking out to their personal tunes or buried in their phones.

Rhys carefully peeled her fingers away from his lips. "I was only going to ask how you can move about within these tight confines?"

At least he'd had the decency to keep his voice down. She eased off of her perched position and set her heels onto the floor. "If you mean this crowded streetcar, it's from habit." She snapped up her index finger in warning. "And that's ALL you'd better've been talkin' 'bout, *cher*. Don't be spoutin' no nonsense here, *oui*? Folks may not look like they're listenin', but ya can't be too sure."

She scanned the faces again and caught a couple sets of peepers quickly flick away. Fingers crossed, she figured the voyeurs were only hoping for a lover's spat. But, unwilling to oblige their desire for a scene, she reined in her temper, waiting patiently by pretending to admire the view while keeping Rhys safely corralled in the corner beside the wheelchair lift.

Every passenger scattered throughout the streetcar continued to stare at him, even after things had quieted down; young and old, all eyes were glued to the glamorous creature at her back. Sensual tension filtered through the air, turning the whole cabin into a hotbed of hungry looks and heavy sighs. She scooted away from a set of questing fingers, only to bump her ass into the cause of the whole commotion.

"End of the line, folks," came the streetcar operator's timely message.

Thank the stars. Cam blew out the breath she'd been holding. Erring on the side of caution, she allowed the other riders to disembark first. Each person who left wore a strange, fuck-drunk grin. Couples walked arm in arm toward their destinations, humming and whistling happily. Just being in his presence had given those near a little id booster shot, including the kindly older lady who'd spilled her sweet tea down the back of Cam's leg.

"What a nice young couple," the older lady murmured, brushing her hand along Rhys's arm before she tottered along her intended path.

Cam groaned, grabbing ahold of Rhys, and joined the remaining passengers on the sidewalk. Rhys apologized to no one in particular as he bumbled to a stop beside her. The gray clouds overhead would do more than just threaten any minute now, and she tugged on her companion's sleeve, tipping her head in their intended direction.

"Let's get a move on, *cher*. Gonna rain soon and don't wanna get soaked."

Rhys nodded and fell into step at her side. The towering fae ambled along, advancing and retreating with an uneven gait.

"And can you tone down the sex vibes?" she said. "I don't want to find myself in the middle of an accidental orgy."

"I thought my powers weren't affecting you." Rhys had practically purred the words into her ear, his lips so close, the warmth of his skin danced along her cheek.

Instinct kicked into gear and she jabbed her elbow into his ribs. "Dang it, *cher*, I mean it." She quickened her pace, wiping the lingering tingles off her face. "Y'ain't affectin' me that much, but can't say the same for the rest of the population, *oui*? And exactly what part of 'no' didn't you get?"

She'd carefully spat out each word, timing each beat with another stride. The sooner she solved this mystery, the sooner she could go back to living in the shadows of blessed anonymity. Passersby *ooh*ed and *ahh*ed in their wake, adding to the occasional whimper and whispers of "Atta girl." She groaned and shifted her gaze to her wide-eyed companion.

In stark contrast, he gaped at everything in innocent exuberance. He touched the bark of the sweet magnolia trees, sniffed in the direction of any open doorway. Cautious, she monitored his exploration from a safe distance, until he almost wandered into someone's home while they sat on the porch. She laughed nervously, dragging Rhys back to the street.

"Tourists, *oui?*" she said and forced a smile, waving to the confused occupants while shoving Rhys toward the tall white building a couple of blocks away.

"Was that not a correct response?" he asked, stumbling on while trying to peer over his shoulder to find her.

She shook her head, sidled around him. "Not quite. We might be friendly here, but you don't just walk uninvited into folk's homes. Gotta be asked. 'Sides"—she paused and pointed to the pristine doors of the well-maintained, white antebellum plantation directly in front of them—"we're here."

"Do you have a plan?"

Cam remained focused on the entrance, frantically trying to formulate her reply. Did she have a plan? A very good question. Too bad she didn't have an answer equally as brilliant. Somewhere inside might be the information she needed to get her life back. So how was she going to find it? Doctors required knowledge beyond her current skill set. Same with nurses. An intern, maybe? Candy striper? Nah ... no way to look into hospital records as a volunteer.

"Camille?"

She drummed her fingers as her mind searched for solutions, the flickering view of the ground soothing and centering. A family member of one of the kids might get info about that one case, but she needed to find the connecting thread between them all. Were they all from one area? Did they all attend the same school? Was it something in the water?

"Camille?"

A gentle tap on her shoulder brought her back to the present.

"Hmm?"

Rhys cocked his head, affixing her with a pensive stare. "I was wondering if you had a plan."

Cam gnawed on her lower lip, praying for divine intervention. At once, inspiration struck, and she shrugged. "Well, it might not be the best idea," she admitted, "but I think I figured something out." Her gaze darted around until it settled on a secluded garden. "Gonna need you to keep watch. I'll be right back."

A strong hand on her arm stopped her, and an excited gleam sparkled in Rhys's soft brown eyes. "Are you going to shift?"

"No." She jerked her arm out his loose grip. "Well, not exactly. It's not a shift; we call it a dance, but ... ooh, just stay over there and make sure no one comes around." She shooed him away, then dashed into the shrubbery. She wouldn't need to make many changes, but the tattoos and piercing would definitely have to go; no way could she sell a CDC executive with more ink on her than a sailor.

Certain she had the necessary privacy, Cam took a deep breath and stripped. Her unique skills did not work on clothes and with the alterations she'd be making, her jeans would cut off the circulation to her legs. She made one final sweep of the area as she stuffed her outfit into her bag, then she held her crouch and closed her eyes. Concentrating, she added some age lines, padded her svelte figure, chopped off about three feet from her hair and four inches from her height. Her arms tingled as her body absorbed the ornate tribal designs, and her silver eyebrow rings bounced off her knee before they landed on the ground.

Her tingling scalp told her the last detail had been locked into place. *Great. Now for the fun part.* She peeled open her eyes and sucked in a sharp breath. Peering over the top of the greenery, she whistled low and hoped Rhys was listening.

"God, I hate this part," she growled to herself, and she called out again, this time a little louder.

CHAPTER 7

hat a wondrous world this place was.

As Rhys explored the open garden decorating the entrance of the hospital, he savored each fresh aroma and novel sensation. Camille had vanished behind an array of well-manicured shrubs and had yet to emerge. The air was thick with the scent of impending rain and he eagerly awaited the downpour. The previous night's shower had only whet his appetite. Water was his element; it revitalized his magicks and soothed his spirit.

As unique as this realm was, though, it did not hold a candle to his homeland. The magnolia trees with their vibrant green leaves and their white flowers' heady fragrance reminded him of the ancient groves surrounding the royal palace. Many of the flora here held strong similarities to those beyond the curtain.

Yet not even the plants in the fae world talked.

Odd whisperings seemed to come from the same area Camille had chosen to use as cover. The sounds came again, and he crept closer. "Camille?"

A head of bouncy dark curls popped over the top of the short hedgerow. "Yes, it's me," she said. "Now get over here. I need your help."

Rhys stared in rapt wonder at the strange person now hunkered behind the shrub. In place of the young woman he'd met, stood an older woman with skin the color of chocolate and eyes like a robin's egg. Not only were her curves more rounded, but they were also rather visible.

"You ... you are in the nude?" He slunk in for a better view.

"Yes." She hissed and quickly thrust up one arm, her other hand acting as a barrier to her bare breasts. He stopped as commanded. "I'm *au naturel*," she said. "I can't do clothes. We can talk more about this later. Right now, I need something to wear."

He tapped his chin, mulling over her odd request. "Shall I return to one of the houses?" he asked, and he turned to begin his new quest for appropriate attire.

She rolled her eyes with a groan, muttering something under her breath as she shook her head. "*Non, cher*. Ain't got no time for that. Just magic me up a business suit." She paused, then added, "Please."

Even her voice had altered, the rich, gravelly tones replaced by a nasally timbre. She'd said they'd speak of this at another time, and he discovered he indeed had many questions for her. "As you wish." His cheeks warmed as he hazarded the next request. "But I will need to see you to, ah, judge the correct sizes."

She narrowed her gaze, muttering as she took to her feet. One glance provided him with all the information he required. "Does the color—"

"Oh, for the love of ... no," she bit out and shrunk back behind her floral barrier, "the color don't matter. It's about to rain and I don't wanna get caught out here naked as a jay bird when it does."

He nodded rapidly and wove his magic into a garment suitable for her needs. She snatched up the clothing, then disappeared once again. He averted his gaze to give her a modicum of privacy. "I was not certain of the style, nor am I well-versed in modern fashion, but—"

"S'all good, *cher*." She stepped out from behind her living dressing room, adjusting the ensemble on her new body. "It only needs to get us in. I got an idea of how to get what we need from there."

Rhys backed up to allow this new version of his fascinating companion to pass by.

"A'ight," she said, shoving her bag into his arms. "Your turn."

He blinked repeatedly. "Beg your pardon?"

She gestured at him, trailing her hand from head to toe. "Can't have you going in looking like that. You'd drive the women in there crazy, and we ain't got all day."

He frowned and glanced down at his attire, which he'd thought was quite similar to those of the people on the earlier conveyance.

She groaned, smacking his arm. "Just make yourself shorter, a little fatter, and not so handsome. We need to not stand out, *oui*?"

Ah. He nodded in understanding before adjusting his glamour, and in the blink of an eye, his perceived appearance had shifted to reflect the requests of his companion. The fact she'd called him handsome hadn't slipped by unnoticed, and he tucked away the compliment for further examination later.

Right now, he opened his arms, eager for her approval. She pursed her lips, studying him, then answered with a shrug and a tip of her chin before continuing on her path. With her stubbier legs, she swayed from side to side, waddling toward the front door. Before grasping the handle, though, she stopped, twitching violently from head to toe, the bizarre tremors skating along her limbs and terminating at her fingertips. She glanced over her shoulder with a bashful expression.

"Is ... is that normal?" he asked, fearing his hushed question would only aggravate her. To his surprise, she answered with another half-hearted shrug and the hint of a smile.

"Pretty much, kinda locks in a big change. C'mon, *cher*. Got work to do." She inclined her head once again toward the three-story building, and he rushed to her side. She gestured to the door, and his chivalrous nature sprung to life. With a flourish, he turned the handle and ushered her inside.

Beyond the glass barrier lay a clean, organized lobby, where a smattering of low-backed chairs had been arranged in cozy couplings. Ivory tiles framed the worn out, faded blue-green carpet, as if protecting it from the elements beyond the walls. Two long corridors spoked out from the central foyer, both disappearing past mazes of cubicles. As Rhys admired the simple architecture, he slung the bulging bag over his head, mimicking Camille's earlier motions.

Undaunted, Camille strode up to the large, rounded desk and rang the small bell.

"Is this the wisest course of action?" Rhys asked, having leaned in, whispering his fears over her direct actions.

A wink.

He frowned, confused. *What did that mean?*

A young female dressed in a smart jacket and matching slacks smiled as she approached. A rectangular tag on her lapel announced her name was Jennifer and, underneath that, the word Receptionist. "Hello," she said. "How may I help you?"

"Hi. Yes. My name is Angela Garçon. I'm from the local office of the Center for Disease Control."

Rhys's jaw popped open at the ease in which the story had fallen from her lips. A sharp pain centered around his ribs, and he glanced down, searching for the cause. Camille had tugged him closer to rummage through her large bag. "We heard you've had an unusual number of flu cases this early in the year. Hang on, *cher*. Got my credentials in here somewhere."

The receptionist waved off her further digging. "Thank God you're here. We've been calling for two days and they kept saying someone was on their way."

Rhys clenched his jaw, holding his tongue behind his teeth. This was a serious matter; truthful deeds would be required. He tapped Camille on the arm, hoping to dissuade her from this charade. Instead, he was relegated to tag behind the two ladies as they hustled down one of the hallways leading away from the central hub. He craned his neck to catch their hurried conversation.

"We are at a loss," Jennifer explained, guiding their twisting path. "None of the standard markers are coming up. The children are of different ages, none of them attend the same school; the only thing they have in common is they aren't responding to any treatment."

Camille asked probing questions as they toured the infirmary, the informational answers lost on him. Rhys stopped to poke his head into one of the rooms. A large metal bed dominated the small space, dwarfing the tiny child tucked beneath the thin white blanket. Hesitant, he crept closer to the sleeping figure. Her features were very similar to Camille's current appearance. Around her, machinery pinged and beeped, nearly masking the young one's labored breathing, and his heart ached to see an innocent robbed of life's joyous and precious moments.

He stepped farther into the room, reaching below the surface, seeking smudges, traces of dark magic that colored the fabric of life. If the illness was designed to attack both human and fae, a trail would lead back to whomever had created it. Yet, when he stared into the beyond, nothing marred the pure space. This was not the illness ravaging his people; it was merely a mortal affliction. *Easy enough to cure.*

"Be at ease, little one." He lightly touched her fevered forehead and willed away the sickness. He watched for another moment, the beeping and whirring pitch of the machinery taking on an even and soothing rhythm.

Armed with his newly discovered knowledge, Rhys slipped out of the room and moved on to the next chamber. There, he found another child, a pale boy slightly older than his previous patient. He boldly approached, certain the youth was fast asleep and, with his arm extended, brushed his outstretched fingertips against an exposed foot. The light contact was enough to act as a conduit for his powers and he grinned to himself.

"Who are you?"

Rhys balked and snapped his gaze up to find a pair of sharp blue eyes peering at him from the head of the bed. Blinking rapidly, he reeled back and bumped into one of the strange rolling carts at the boy's bedside. Apologies tumbled from his lips as he reached for the escaping table, but instead of stopping the offending device, he managed to knock it farther across the room.

"MOM!"

The howling call drew the attention of every person within earshot. Rhys backed toward the exit, nearly tearing off the thin, hanging curtain, and landed in the hallway in an ungraceful heap. Camille poked her head out of an opening a few feet from his current position. Astonishment had screwed up her cocoa complexion. Another figure dressed in a long white coat soon added his head to the odd totem pole. Their tour guide slid in between. Confused, she drew her eyebrows together, deliberately swinging her gaze from Rhys to Camille.

"What are you doing in this patient's room?" she asked.

Rhys stammered and attempted to climb back to his feet, all the while hoping for a glib response to Jennifer's question.

"Dang it all." Camille stepped out and guided Rhys to standing. "You need to learn to keep up." She dusted off the back of his jacket, slapping at some dirt only she could see. "I swear, breaking in a new secretary is harder than teaching a cat to play bridge. Come on, Bradley, we've taken enough of this nice lady's time." Camille's less-than-gentle hand along his back guided him away quicker than his legs could manage. "Thank you again, *cher*. We'll be in touch," she said, waving to no one in particular behind her, pointedly ignoring the requests to stop.

As she snuck around him, she muttered the strangest command, before dashing full speed toward the door.

"Run!"

CHAPTER 8

Camille swore under her breath, wishing she spoke more than two languages. She recalled hearing that Russian had some pretty mean curse words, but she'd never quite made it to that part of the world.

Everything had been going so well. Jennifer had introduced her to the lead doctor on the kids' cases, and even though her knowledge of the medical field was limited to "Grey's Anatomy" and reruns of "ER," she'd known enough to translate some of his Latin. He'd been beginning to make sense, when a loud crash had grabbed everyone's attention. She should have known something would go sideways when she noticed her knight absent during the biology lesson. She'd guided their hasty retreat to the most crowded part of the hospital parking lot to cower in the midday shadows until the security guards had given up the chase.

Hiding behind a van in a nearby alley, she jammed her legs back into her jeans, happy to once again be in her own skin. "So close," she mumbled. *Dammit all.* She jerked her gaze about, searching for a dry spot on the ground. A new string of profanities picked up where the other left off as she leaned her back against the damp bricks and yanked on her socks and boots. The slick, uneven wall bit into her bare skin and dug into her bra straps, giving her another reason to be pissed off.

No matter how she spun it, she ended up livid. She forced her fingers to knot the misbehaving laces before she kicked off the wall to drag on her rumpled tank.

"Dammit, dammit, dammit." Fully clothed, she marched straight up to Rhys, stopping only when the space between them had disappeared. "I was this close to getting the answers I needed." She shoved her hand in front of his nose, her thumb and forefinger a scant breath apart. "This close. Can't I leave you alone for a minute?"

Now she was stuck. No new leads, no new direction. She tossed her hands up, frustrated, and stormed away, lest she do something she might truly regret. *He means well,* her good-natured self argued. A final drag of her left hand along the length of her right arm returned her cherished tattoos and she slipped back into her light jacket, scoffing as she argued back, *Yeah, and the check's in the mail.*

A gentle hand on her arm stalled her escape. "But those children were not going to help us in our quest," he said, both calm and confusion blending in his tone.

"Really, Dr. Kildare?" She spun around, fumbling with the zipper's base. "How do you figure that?" She focused on the two willful bits of metal refusing to meet, angry at the world.

"Because I healed them."

"YOU WHAT?" She snapped her head up. "You're joking, right?"

The confused puppy look reappeared on his face, his eyebrows tugging together as his head cocked slightly. "Was that wrong of me to do?"

She sputtered, searching for the right response to his innocent query. Again, she flung her arms skyward. "Well, no, but people don't just ... just get better overnight."

Pacing gave her body purpose as her mind sifted through the ramifications of his actions. She hastily checked her watch, then pointed her toes on a reverse course. Once the doctors had realized two of their patients no longer exhibited any symptoms, perhaps they could find a vaccine to help others afflicted by this new flu. Or maybe they'd find nothing at all, since magic left no lingering evidence in the human world. Either way, two families would be taking their beloved children home tonight, celebrating the miraculous recovery. No doubt, they'd be thanking God, too.

Her gaze slid over to the sulking cause for the divine rebound, as he fell into step beside her. Knight of the Lesser Court of the Fae. He'd only been responding to a cry of those in need. Could she really fault him for that?

"It is simply what I do," he replied quietly. "Are you cross with me?" She hated the timidity in his voice. It wasn't fair of her to expect him to know all the rules in this world, especially during his first tour of duty in the mortal realm.

Huffing out her tangle of emotions, she dropped her head and shook it slowly from side to side. "*Chagren.* I'm sorry. I'm not mad. But now I'm no further along than I was this morning."

The large presence at her side paused, another light touch on her arm drawing her once again to a halt. "That is not necessarily true," he stated.

She trailed her gaze up to meet his soft brown eyes. While she had danced, transforming piece by piece back to her comfortable self, he merely blinked, and the glamour returned him to all his splendor.

She sighed, rested her fist against her hip. "Why do you say that, *cher*?"

Rhys smiled softly, the tender expression reserved more for pets rather than for lovers. "Do you not understand?" he said. "I *healed* the children. It is what I do. I am a Knight, and it is my duty."

"You already said that, but what does ... oh." Understanding washed over her like a cool rain on a hot summer day. Of course. If the children had been infected with the same disease attacking the fae, his magicks would have been useless. "Now, just hang on a second," she said. "When you say 'knight,' what exactly does that mean?"

He placed his right fisted hand over his heart. "I swore an oath to save life."

Save life. Two simple words that held a much different connotation. "So, you're a ... a healer?"

Rhys dipped his chin. "My magicks are able to cure any ailment not born of magic. Why?" he asked. "What else would a knight do?"

"Around these parts, they usually slay dragons and ride around in armor, rescuing damsels in distress. But I get the saving people part. Guess I didn't think of a knight as anything other than, well ... a knight."

"Do I disappoint you?" She cringed inwardly at his childlike question. He'd only been following his duty. Who was she to judge?

She reached out and touched his hand. "Nah," she said. "S'all good." She lingered a moment before adding, "Thank you for helping those kids back there."

Now I know why he was sent, she mused as she continued her journey back to the streetcar stop.

By learning the sick kids were not a part of the mystery, she could rule out any other news about a flu. The earlier downpour while they had been playing detective thinned out the black clouds overhead, and spears of sun warmed pockets of the world.

Snippets of music flowed out of half-open windows, ranging from bass-thumping hip-hop to live sessions of zydeco. Cam closed her eyes and fell into the rhythmic trance of her city. The heart of New Orleans lay in its music, the blood pumped by the horn of Louis Armstrong and the voice of Ella Fitzgerald, and serenity filled her spirit as she bounced along to the beat, her pace shifting with each new song.

Even though Rhys had cloaked his otherworldliness, waves of raw sensual power still slipped through, affecting any hormonally active human within arm's reach, making their return trip increasingly uncomfortable. Any pedestrians they passed by whimpered and Cam groaned in sympathy.

"You are in a surprisingly cheerful mood," he remarked, oblivious to his effect on the passersby.

She chuckled at his odd statement and, with a half-shrug, she jammed her hands into her pockets. "Just listenin', *cher*. Just listenin'." Her fingers brushed against her ring and a pair of small hoops and, with a shake of her head, she traced her right brow ridge in search of the two openings. It would be a bitch to have to get pierced again, but it seemed luck was on her side for the moment. She fiddled with the locking balls and deftly slid each ring into place as they continued on their trek back toward home.

Whistling along to the miscellaneous music, she slipped the broad ring onto her right middle finger and dragged in a deep, cooling breath. This was why she'd always found her way back to Louisiana. Here, she was home.

A commotion disrupted her reverie. Sirens wailed louder and louder through the jazz, and at the corner across the way, a knot of people had gathered. One person split off from the group to flag down the approaching ambulance. *Convenient,* she thought. *At least the ride to the hospital won't be too expensive.* She continued on, yet a glimpse of scuffed tan-and-white shoes of the downed victim caught her eye.

"Deacon?" she whispered.

Without a word, Cam grabbed Rhys's sleeve and dashed with him to the other side of the street. She elbowed her way closer, intent on the clamor of voices. She picked out Rhys's quizzical tone but waved off his interference.

"Never seen anything like it."

"He was just walking, then dropped to the ground, flopping like a beached fish."

"Didn't say nothing. Just fell over and died."

Too many versions of what happened to sift through, yet one factor remained the same: there was neither a perpetrator nor a crime; most murmured theories circled back to heart attack or seizure. Cam kept her attention on the man on the ground, careful to keep out from underfoot while the paramedics scurried around him, checking for a pulse and other vital readings.

"Do you know him?"

She acknowledged Rhys's question with a nod but did not shift her focus. "Deacon was one of my regulars. He was a nice enough guy. Part of the Tuesday crew." Why had that particular band of hooligans stuck to that moniker when they darkened her bar practically every night? She didn't know more than his first name and his preference for Grey Goose over Russian Standard. He must have had a job to afford a three-drink-a-night habit, but she'd never deigned to ask.

"When did you see him last?"

His simple question yanked her back into the present.

"Saw him last..." A piece slowly fell into place. "He was there last night," she said. "I remember showing him the picture Zacarias gave me. He saw you both."

CHAPTER 9

Zacarias strode around the sparsely furnished dwelling. He had to hand it to her ... she was smart. Nothing in the scattered keepsakes offered a clue about her true self. A handful of stock images in unremarkable frames decorated random wall spaces, the faces bearing enough of a likeness to fool any glances. Mementos from typical vacations littered bookshelves, hung from the bathroom vanity mirror. To the casual onlooker, Camille Anaïs Delacroix was a normal girl in her mid- to late-twenties working as a barkeep to pay the bills until something better came along.

"Very clever," he murmured appreciatively as he traced his fingertips along the homespun comforter covering the princess bed in the back bedroom. Through this light contact, he glimpsed her as she'd appeared only hours ago. Her last moments spent there had been filled with sorrow. He frowned, flattening his palm against the quilt to discover more. Memories of her parents and their stern warnings about dealing with the fae had troubled her dreams.

And something else....

The corners of his lips tugged up as he gathered hungered thoughts directed toward him. So, she was interested after all. He withdrew his hand, secreting away this newly acquired information, and returned to the living room.

The sun had long since gone down in the west, and rain sweetened the air. Zacarias settled into the chair farthest from her front door, grateful for the cleansing damp. Seconds ticked by on her simple wall clock, and with each subsequent sound, his patience waned.

At last, the door handle rattled and the door was flung open. An odd silence hung over the pair as they shuffled inside, bedraggled and soaked, with the lingering scent of heavy spices and hot oil following in her wake, alluding to a quick meal of some fried monstrosity. Why so many humans enjoyed their food prepared in such a flavor-destroying method was beyond him. At the soft shut of the door, Zacarias decided to make his presence known.

"I trust this delay means you have discovered the information I need."

Camille yelped, her gaze darting around until she spied him in the corner. Anger quickly replaced her momentary surprise, and she hurled her keys in his general direction.

"How the hell did you get into my apartment?"

Zacarias easily captured the flying jangle of metal and set them down onto the table beside him. He rose out of the overstuffed chair, sighing, and sauntered out of the shadows. "Your boss was kind enough to let me in," he said. "After all, I do have a message for your, ah, cousin." He arched one brow as the last word fell from his tongue.

Rhys blanched, turning the color of cold oatmeal before stalking over, confident and proud, to stand nose to nose with him. "Deliver your message and be gone, tyrant."

Zacarias bared his teeth, hands fisting at his sides. "You stand before your betters. Do not forget your place, cur."

"Oh, hell no." Camille shouldered herself between Zacarias and his target. "Both of you," she snapped, "dial down the testosterone or I swear to Christ, I will toss both your asses outta here." Her arms shook with the effort to separate them. "Dammit all, I mean it. Back. Off." She slammed her foot to the ground and, with a final, herculean push, she shoved them apart. Her ragged breathing added a strange, syncopated harmony to the snarls and growls from the opposite sides of the room.

Zacarias paced in a tight circle, glaring daggers at the meddling fae. Out of all the options, he was the best?

Time pulled the silence along, until only the thrumming of the rain on the windowpanes disrupted the calm.

"This," she panted out, gaze fixed on the floor, "is not helping anything."

She did have a point. Zacarias stared until Rhys broke, shifting his gaze away. He turned his attention to Camille, who raised her head.

"Now," she went on, "I honestly don't care about who has the bigger dick." At this, she paused awkwardly. A curious flicker of interest flashed in her rich green eyes but vanished with a rapid shake of her damp hair, and Zacarias filed away this nugget for later contemplation. "But y'all need to set aside any crap you're hanging on to and learn to play nice. Got it?"

Quiet again crept into the room. "Got it?" she repeated, a little louder this time. Her face swiveled back and forth between them, and Rhys closed his eyes, dipped his chin. Zacarias rolled his eyes at the regal gesture, then stalked toward the partial wall separating the kitchen from the rest of the house.

He glared at the knight, gnashing his teeth at the strange surge of jealousy. Granted, he and Rhys had never had many dealings within their prospective courts. Rhys stayed primarily in the calling of the queen's half-sister, but he knew of the man's proclivity for inept interference. This was no rival, merely an obstacle.

"Did you find any new information?"

Camille huffed, blowing away a stray swirl of her raven-black hair. "Yeah," she said. "Found out that magic cures the common cold."

Zacarias narrowed his gaze, folding his arms across his chest. "And what exactly does that mean?"

"It means the lead I thought I had this morning didn't pan out, okay?" She shouldered past him, peeling off her sopping jacket. The white tank top underneath left little to his imagination, including the state of her toned, flat abs and the shade of her pale pink bra. "Turns out, it was only a new case of the flu. Mr. Chivalrous here"—she jerked her thumb toward Rhys as she retrieved a towel from the small closet beside the bathroom—"decided to swoop in and save the whole day."

Zacarias scoffed, shaking his head. "You are sent here to redeem yourself but I see you are as much of a bumbling mess in this realm as you are in ours."

Rhys flew at him once again. "I sensed no trace of magic, so I took the risk. My duty is to preserve life. Why are *you* here?"

Camille stepped between them for a second time, and Zacarias inhaled deep, pulling in her scent. Her anger had soured the underlying hints of jasmine and sweet rain, darkening the light fragrance. Faint traces of her heady fragrance clung to the damp cloth that pressed into his chest, yet her eyes were focused on Rhys. Did she have feelings for this oaf?

"Now I mean it. You two, cut it out." She gave them an additional shove, and Zacarias stalked toward the couch. "Dammit all. Y'all need to quit this machismo shit or I'll throw the pair of you out the friggin' window."

Camille swung her head back and forth between him and Rhys, quiet as though she dared either of them to speak, and Zacarias dipped his chin, hoping to hide his appreciative smirk. Rhys bowed, placing his fisted right hand over his heart. Another oath of fealty? This should be interesting.

"Please tell me the day was not a total loss." Zacarias stated, staring at the nauseating scene as he lowered himself onto the cushions. "We are running out of time." He squeezed the words passed the knot in his throat, remembering the visceral and all-consuming grief in the eyes of his queen. The princess's condition had worsened since yesterday, and unless he found the cure within the next two days, she would surely perish.

The silence that followed drew his gaze back into the present of the room. Camille rubbed the nape of her neck, the gesture speaking of either fatigue or stress. His fingers itched, and he fought off the urge to take over massaging. He'd only make such a move once he was certain it would be received with enthusiasm. The longer he pondered the feel of her flesh beneath his palms, however, the more constraining his jeans became.

"Not sure if it means anything," her gravelly voice cut through his fantasies, "but Deacon, one of my regulars at the bar, just died on the street as we were heading back here."

Zacarias tugged his eyebrows together. "Died? How?"

She responded with a half-hearted shrug and crossed to the simple black wooden coat rack beside the front door to hang the damp jacket to dry. "Don't rightly know yet. People around said it looked like he was having a heart attack, or a seizure, or something like that." She moved gracefully through the space, fairly dancing around the spartan furniture before disappearing into the bedroom. "Don't think he was that old," she called back, "but I've never been a good judge in that field." Her voice echoed off the walls, and she returned, yanking on a dry, oversize shirt. *What a shame.* He was rather enjoying seeing her parade around in the wet T-shirt.

"Was he of ill health?" Rhys piped in, stealing the question that should have been his. He'd been so distracted by Camille's sweet, naïve seduction, he was losing sight of his true purpose. Digging his fingers into his palm, Zacarias used the sting to center his rebellious mind.

Camille shrugged, rolling up the sleeves that engulfed her arms. "Well, he was a regular and did like his drink, so I don't think he was the healthiest of people. But," she paused, tucking the corner of her lip between her teeth, "he was at the bar last night. Not that others weren't there too, but he did see both of you show up."

"It could be simple coincidence," he said and chewed on the idea a bit more, his original assumption seeming weak. "But we shouldn't completely rule it out as something more."

"My thoughts, too." Camille moved toward the kitchen. "The standard crew was there last night. I'll keep an eye out for anyone else to drop dead." She opened the refrigerator, removed three tall green bottles, and returned to the living room. "Have there been more cases in your world?"

Using the thick titanium band on her right middle finger as an impromptu bottle opener, she snapped off the metal caps with practiced ease and handed out the drinks. Zacarias accepted the offering and gave the contents a cautionary sniff. Beer. He'd know that aroma anywhere. Crisp and hoppy, it would be cool on the tongue and light on the palate. *And it might derail the evening into a drunken debacle*, he mused.

His kind generally did not mix well with human alcohol, the dizzying factor dangerous at times if not kept in check. He glanced sidelong at Rhys, gauging the knight's response. Zacarias was certain Camille would not be affected greatly by one drink, given her current occupation. He could be mistaken, but he highly doubted it. She'd been living in the mortal realm for centuries. Certainly, she was accustomed to the volatile substance.

Rhys tipped back the bottle, then promptly sprayed the contents of his mouth across the room. "This is not the same drink as yesterday," he sputtered, dragging his hand past his lips to remove the lingering evidence.

Camille wiped off the sleeve of her shapeless heather gray shirt, shaking her head. "Dang, *cher*. Didn't know you couldn't handle your alcohol." She chuckled, then plopped down into the nearest chair, remaining out of arm's reach from either Rhys or himself. Clever indeed.

Zacarias lifted the bottle in a toast. "Many of my brethren cannot handle their liquor." He smirked, the gauntlet well and truly thrown down. Rhys glared, yet set down the drink, refusing to take the bait. *Pity.* Zacarias took a sip, savored the mouthful before swallowing it. Precisely as he'd predicted, the beverage was passable. Not terribly flavorful, but it did quench his immediate thirst.

A tapping on his spiritual shoulder reminded him of his duties, his queen's voice forlorn in his mind as it begged for a solution. So, ignoring his more primal desires, he returned to the task at hand.

"What other courses of action are you planning for tomorrow?"

He shifted his gaze to his silent hostess, who finished off the last of her beer and retrieved Rhys's still-full container. "Rhys said he detected some trace of magic near where we found Deacon, but—"

"And you failed to mention this until now, why?" Zacarias roared, sitting bolt upright. How much time had that buffoon wasted before revealing this crucial nugget?

Camille waved him back while Rhys shot to his feet. "Because the effects were not a strong enough source to have been the cause of his death."

"And you would know that how, dog?" Zacarias snarled and slowly rose from the couch. "I don't think you would know true power if it appeared before your very nose."

An odd feminine growl filled the room, disgust and aggravation having blended into the guttural sound. "You know, I'm through playing referee." Camille joined in their posturing poses before finally turning her stare directly toward him. Anger and exhaustion, and perhaps even a dash of passion, burned deep in her fiery jade eyes. He filed the hope away. "Even if there was anything more than a small bit," she said, "the body was cold dead when we got there." And her voice caught, tripping over the loss of an acquaintance.

Zacarias immediately regretted his churlish behavior. He stilled, lost in the intensity of her eyes, then he dipped his chin to hold the tentative connection a moment longer.

"I am sorry for the loss of your companion, Camille," he said, hoping she sensed the honesty in his words. But ever the nuisance, his rival attempted to interrupt things, stepping in close and dropping a possessive arm across her shoulders.

Her eyes flared. Was she surprised or pleased by the attentions? Zacarias was not certain ... until she flew out of the knight's loose embrace.

"Dammit all, Rhys, I'm not some friggin' prize for y'all to be fightin' over." And she stalked away, soon followed by the clattering of the empty bottle as it bounced into some receptacle. He had caught a quick dash of her hand across her eyes before she fled and was touched by her show of emotion. "And to answer your original question," she added, "I was planning on going to the police station tomorrow to see what I can find out about Deacon's death. He was someone I did consider a friend, so maybe they'll give me something more than what I'd hear on the news." She stopped at her bedroom door, fingers hovering above the rounded knob before she spun about with a flourish to face him and his rival. "Now, I'm going to bed. I don't care who sleeps where, but I know for sure ain't neither of y'all comin' through this door."

The hinge squeaked and groaned before the final slam had punctuated her exit.

Zacarias paused before shifting his gaze toward the errant knight, while a soft click filled the silence. Rhys jutted out his chin as if daring him to knock it back into place, and he folded his arms across his chest.

I do not have time for this.

"Your bed awaits, sire." Zacarias gestured grandly toward the narrow couch, and before the man could respond, he slipped into the nearest shadow and departed.

Besides—he chuckled softly—*I have better accommodations awaiting me.*

CHAPTER 10

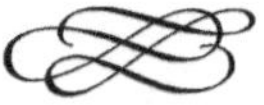

"Camille..."

The tempting voice danced across her skin; a mink glove promising earth-shattering passion. Her gaze darted around the foggy alley in search of the tantalizing speaker. From the mist rose a pair of electric blue eyes—haunting, captivating. Cam gasped, entranced, as Zacarias strode forward. He stalked toward her. His jet black button-down shirt hung open, and the lean muscles revealed rippled with each of his predatory strides. She trembled in eager anticipation. Would he be caring and compassionate as a lover, or would he take only what he wanted and leave her begging for more?

A slow smile curved the corners of his firm mouth, and with one final move, he stood before her. The heat from his nearness warmed her cheek even as she looked away from the enticing sight. *This is a dream*, she rationalized.

He chuckled, and powerless to resist, she climbed her gaze upwards. Chiseled pecs gave way to broad shoulders, and higher still she drew her eyes to his dusty blond hair that brushed just past the base of his neck. Her fingers itched to test the texture.

Don't worry, it's only a dream.

"Is that what you want to believe?" Zacarias purred, his breath tickling the top of her head, and she shivered in response.

"It's the only possible explanation." Her raspy voice had cracked as need thickened in her throat.

"Then touch me. Prove this all to be an illusion."

His chest rose and fell, beckoning her on to a more tactile examination. Her hand twitched while she mentally fought against his alluring offer, hesitating, unwilling to break the spell. She held her outstretched fingers a whisper away from his bare skin.

"Can't I just enjoy this flight of fantasy?" Resigned, she closed her eyes, lids fluttering down, her heart fearing the disappointment of discovering this was all in her imagination. Her body, on the other hand, had something else in mind and closed the final distance between them. Heat sparked in the center of her palm, and she swore a steady pulse beat against her hand.

Cool air kissed her from head to toe, and her eyes snapped open. The red brick walls had vanished as she now stood on some distant shore. Fine sand slipped between her bare toes. Panic-stricken, she glanced down at the tiniest excuse for a swimsuit covering her body. Two minuscule triangles of bright fuchsia fabric strung together by a mere cat's whisker covered her nipples, while a third swath and some thin ribbon kept her lady parts barely hidden from prying eyes.

She squeaked, hands splayed out to make up for the lack of material. "Now, just hang on a second!" she yelled. "If this was my dream, I sure as hell wouldn't be on a deserted island in a friggin' pink bikini."

Waves washed along the shore, and she could have sworn she heard a devilish laugh carried along by the ocean breeze. *Her* dream. She focused on the thought and took ownership. In the blink of an eye, gone was the garish pink, and in its place swathed a soothing tropical green suit with a bit more coverage. Pleased with her newfound control, Cam lowered her arms.

A presence moved in behind her with a soft hiss of sand at her back. Her breath quickened, but she did not budge. Nearer and nearer the footfalls came. The tiny hairs on her nape stood at attention, as if straining with all their might to make contact with the hot-blooded fae she knew stood only inches away.

Dream. Remember it's not real.

"So certain and so eager to dismiss this. Tell me, my ever-changing one ... will you run from this dream?"

Zacarias. Grand Enforcer of the High Court of the Fae. Current thorn in her side. And fucking sex god whom she wanted more than she cared to admit. Electricity fired through her veins, and heat blossomed between her thighs. Never before had anticipation made her so wet and horny.

She wished her mind could convince her body of this make-believe scenario, but her body was too spun up, and when his chest pressed against her back, she groaned, delighting in the solid connection. He wound an arm around her shoulders, drew her in close.

A heady growl spilled down her bare skin as he nuzzled her hair and, intoxicated by his erotic teasing, she lolled her head to the side, dizzy from want. He licked and nipped his way along her throat, and her legs buckled. She dug her short nails into the meaty safety band holding her in place, desperate for an anchor in this rising storm, then she rolled through her spine, reveling in the contact, even if it was only in her mind. The rough denim scratched at her bare skin, adding to the tantalizing sensations.

She only needed to wonder about the whereabouts of his other strong hand for a mere second; as if by magic, it splayed across her bare midriff, sparking fireworks behind her eyes and between her legs. He continued the exploration, tracing the line down toward her hipbone, and she rubbed her thighs together, increasing the damp and stoking the flames within her blood. With a wicked laugh, he slid the stringy floss away, toying with her for a moment longer before slipping two fingers inside her hot core.

She threw back her head, moaning in ecstasy. Her hips bucked wildly, eager and ready to reach the peak of pleasure. But he allowed her no wiggle room; he held her tight in the solid cage of his embrace, refusing to let her go, and with aching patience, he withdrew his invasion, lightly stroking the edges of her sheath. She refused to beg, yet her body sought more. She'd been alone for far too long and she'd almost forgotten the all-consuming fire of sex.

Almost.

The chiseled planes of his chest were a delicious backrest for her, strong and unyielding. She writhed, urging him on, ground her hips against his crotch, desperate for more friction. The bulge in his pants was massive, and she could make out the thick, toe-curling length of his cock from the crease nestled against her ass. Yet, he made no move to unleash the beast. Instead, he was content to torment her with merciless teasing, dipping only his fingertips inside her before pulling out once again. Over and over, he denied her the release she desperately craved.

Zacarias whispered something into her ear, the language unfamiliar, but the hungered growl that tickled her skin was obvious. She had only a moment to process the thought, before he plunged his long fingers deep inside her, his knuckles knocking against the base of her pelvis.

At once, she cried out in ecstasy, overcome by the swift and sudden shift, and only the vice-like grip of her inner thighs on his hand and the strength of his arm around her shoulders had stopped her from melting into the sand beneath her feet. Balanced on the precipice of an orgasm, she drew in a deep breath to prepare for the oncoming storm.

He dragged his tongue along her tense neck, grip tightening, and she moaned, encouraging him to make good on his delicious offer. He drove her closer to that perfect peak, his hard and fast strokes powerful and relentless, and her wish was finally granted. As he scissored his long fingers sunk deep in her quivering channel, he circled his thumb against her sensitive clit. She bucked against his body, fire dancing through her blood as she rode the waves of pleasure.

Dream time held no meaning; it could have lasted for two minutes or two years. Either way, she didn't care. Instead, she panted, sucking down imaginary air while she reveled in the tingling aftermath of her release. Her body shuddered as he withdrew his hand, and she uttered an unladylike whimper.

Her partner placed a soft, almost loving kiss against her throat, and she paused, surprised by the tender intimacy.

"Now think what I could have done, *ma minette*, had you unlocked your bedroom door."

Cam gasped and jackknifed off the bed, the sweat-dampened sheets sticky against her skin.

CHAPTER 11

The cold shower designed to punish Camille's rebellious body definitely got her mind back to business. She'd been so overwhelmed by Zacarias's sudden appearance in her apartment, the shock must have burrowed its way into her subconscious and driven her dreams into an uncomfortably horny place. That had to be the explanation; she staunchly refused to believe otherwise. The argument between the voices in her head continued as she dressed in her standard fare: a white tank and a pair of close-fitting jeans.

So perfect was his seduction, it had to have been a dream. No way would someone as arrogant and demanding as the Grand Enforcer be that tender and compassionate in the bedroom. Her imagination and her sex-starved state had gotten the better of her. She wanted a hot night with a man who'd fulfill her desires. That was it. So, nothing more than her overactive imagination ... because, in truth, anything other than that would have been a violation. She'd ordered both of them to stay out of her bedroom, had even slammed the door to make it perfectly clear. Apparently, she'd need to add her imaginary bedroom to the next nightly edict.

It had only been a dream. That was all. Nothing more than a vivid, erotic fantasy. No harm; no foul.

She repeated the mantra, forcing her mind to alter the memory of her nighttime visitation, and maybe if she said it often enough, she might even convince her hopeful heart of the futility of any relations with the man.

Not a man.

The truth of those three words stopped her in her tracks. Zacarias wasn't simply a man. He was more—he was a fae, an immortal creature of myth and legend, one of such cruel beauty, humans were said to have gone mad after only one touch. Others were rumored to have died in the throes of unbelievable ecstasy.

Her hand hovered above the handle of the door connecting her bedroom to the rest of the apartment, specifically the living room. What would she do if Zacarias waited on the other side? Would she yell at him, incensed by his invasion? Ignore him and pretend the dream didn't happen? Run into his arms and beg for him to finish what she'd imagined he started?

Huffing out a frustrated breath, Cam gripped the knob and yanked the door open. At once, her gaze darted around the room, but Zacarias was nowhere to be found. Only Rhys was visible, leaning over the small dinette set in her postage-stamp-sized dining room, barefoot, wearing jeans and another sleeveless T-shirt. He hummed half to himself while he set down two plates loaded with a healthy heaping of breakfast goodies. The eggs steamed away happily as he turned his head toward her.

"Good morning, Camille." He rose nobly, tipping his chin. "I trust you slept well. I ... I took the liberty of fixing a morning meal for you. I do hope you approve." And he gestured to the banquet complete with a carafe of coffee and a delicate single white rose as a centerpiece. Hesitating for only a moment, Rhys stepped up behind one of the chairs and pulled it out for her in true chivalrous fashion.

She blinked, reengaging her brain, and nodded in response, smiling at his proper manners. "Yeah, *merci, cher*. Looks good." She crossed to the cozy table and accepted the offered seat while her stomach growled loudly at the heavenly smells wafting up from the loaded plate. She chuckled. "Well, maybe it looks a little better than good."

Rhys beamed at her weak compliment and joined her at the table. "It was the least I could do after you defended me last night."

Cam tugged her eyebrows together, a forkful of deliciousness inches away from her mouth as she smiled shyly. "Don't be thanking me for too much now, *cher*. I just didn't want the pair of you to tear up my place." She dove into the meal, dismissing the rest of the topic. No sense in letting it get cold. Besides, she was eager to avoid any further talk regarding the previous evening.

The eggs were fluffy and flavorful, with a hint of rosemary blended in with the nutty bite of Parmesan cheese. Perfectly golden-brown toast cut in precise triangles sat on their own plate, butter coating each piece from edge to edge. A full pot of freshly brewed coffee and a colorful bowl of strawberries and blueberries completed the feast. She glanced over at her fridge. Did she even have fruit? Though she feared for the state of her kitchen, she ignored the urge to peek over the counter to see the degree of possible devastation. Who knows? Maybe he was a conscientious cook and did all the dishes.

He is a fae, for Pete's sake. He probably magicked the whole thing without blinking an eye.

As the food disappeared off her plate, she soon realized she didn't care how it had made it to her table. She was just grateful for the warm meal.

A heavy weight pressed on the top of her head—*Crap*—and she swallowed the mouthful before glancing up sheepishly at her curious guest. "Sorry, *cher*. Guess I'm so used to eating by myself I forgot how to behave when I actually have company."

Rhys shook his head, an odd twinkle in his soft brown eyes. "I'm simply glad the meal met with your approval," he said and winked at her, then returned to his own food.

Why was he so damned polite? Both of the males who'd barged into her life were so similar, except ... Rhys was everything Zacarias wasn't. Power oozed off the pair of them like an expensive cologne, both tempting and mouthwatering. Yet, where Zacarias was pompous and overbearing, Rhys was considerate and caring. Her mind jumped back to her illicit dream, and she quickly rethought her opinion of Zacarias.

"Is something wrong?" Rhys's cautious question had dragged her back to the kitchen table. Concern radiated from his deep topaz eyes, and when he reached across the narrow span, warmth from his fingers brushed along her skin. But before he could make contact, Cam jumped to her feet. Distance. She needed distance. Her body was still on edge, primed for action in the afterglow of her erotic fantasy, and she didn't want to make any rash decisions in real time.

"No, I'm fine," she said, heading toward the kitchen with her dishes. "Wait." She turned to face him. Something about what Zacarias said flashed into her mind. "Why you?"

Rhys blinked repeatedly while he did his best impression of a dying goldfish. "I-I do not know-"

Cam lifted her hand to pause his forming excuse. "You didn't just volunteer. It's more than that." His gaze hit the floor. "C'mon. I won't judge."

"I am a Knight of the Fourth Order," he said, pride and pain coloring his voice. "If I am not able to aide you in this task and find the cure, I will be stripped of my title and cast out of my order."

Damn. That put a new spin on things. "Well, looks like we both have a dog in this fight after all. Okay, we gotta get moving soon. Got an idea, and I'll need to hit the police station for it." Prepared for a disaster in the sink, she was mildly surprised to find a stack of pots and pans neatly angled in the dish rack. She quickly washed her plate and fork and added them to the drying pile.

She was right on all counts. Her plan was to talk to the local officers to see what she could find out about Deacon's death. Simple enough, and she might even get a clue or two in the process. After that, she'd do some digging with the other barflies at her place. Maybe someone knew more about Deacon in life. *Any port in a storm.*

Lost in her plotting, she turned away from the sink, only to slam right into Rhys's chest. Reflexes kicked in and she squeezed her arms between them, palms splayed against the thin fabric covering a set of solid pecs.

"Will you allow me to show you the depths of my gratitude, Camille?" His face descended, lips parted, and the kiss caught her unprepared. The press of his mouth against hers didn't immediately stir up any wild passions, though neither did it make her want to retreat. With some practice, he might become a halfway decent kisser. Firm, yet cautious and tentative, he traced the seam of her lips with his tongue, while he crowded her into the corner, where he cupped her face and pulled her close enough for her to feel the growing size of his interest. That did it.

"Dammit, Rhys," she mumbled against his lips. With a hard shove, she broke the seal of their mouths, bumping her lower back against the edge of the counter in her escape and, stalking away, ran a shaky hand through her hair. "When I said no, I meant it. Why can't I get you to understand? Do I have to spell it out for you? This ... all this. I've spent my whole life staying away from the magical world. Now, after two"—she stabbed her fingers into a V as punctuation—"two friggin' days, the pair of you have screwed up my good record. And gotta tell you, I really don't like being up to my neck in nymphomaniacal fae."

She added the required choreography in the prerequisite places, her arms flailing about with all the grace of an inflatable tube man. The urge to smack him with each movement was tempting, but that would put her within his reach, so she opted for a short walk out of the cramped kitchen. "What is this obsession with you and sex anyway? Is that what you think all humans do?"

"Is it not?"

She threw her hands up, his honest inquiry angering her more than his unexpected pass. "No, genius, it's not. They work, they laugh, they cry...." She snatched up her deep cherry Doc Martens and, perched on the corner of the library table by the front door, laced up the worn leather boots. "They drink, they ... they go bowling." She took to her feet, grabbed her jacket off the decorative coat rack, and jammed her arms into the still-damp sleeves. "And I'm only half-human, as you are all so fond of reminding me. Now, if you don't mind," she declared, "I am going to see if I can find some answers to get all you damned fairies out of my life."

With an angered yank, she pulled open the door, only to have it bounce shut. Rhys braced one arm against the wood, and she snapped her gaze up. A fraction of her rage dissipated, and she dialed down the attitude when she met his guileless, apologetic eyes. Sorrow poured out of him at an alarming rate. Even though his frame practically blocked out all of the light from the living room, the man standing before her was truly a babe in the woods; an innocent walking around in a sex-god suit.

"All of my knowledge regarding the human realm has been about physical intimacy. I assumed their ways would have permeated your behaviors. It appears I was mistaken and have much to learn."

"Gee? Ya think?" She offered him a half-smirk for his partial apology, arms folding across her chest. "If you'd been listening, I've been trying to tell you that people are ... complicated. They aren't the two-dimensional beings you guys think they are."

A distant memory flitted through her mind: She and her mother sat along the banks of the Huveaune River, watching her father fish for their dinner. Curious, she'd asked her mother about the immortal world and why she'd given it all up. At first, she'd believed the question would remain unanswered, the silence between them so deep, the only sound the babbling of the crisp waters.

Her mother rarely told Cam about her other life, and even then, she only learned information deemed necessary for her to understand and control her magicks. So when her mother did speak, the words stayed with her.

"The beauty of a rose is judged naught by the days of its bloom, it is in the joy the flower leaves long after its short existence has ended."

Cam blinked rapidly, shrugging off the prophetic remembrance, and sighed. "Can I trust you not to try to hump my leg every time I turn around? 'Cuz I'd rather have an extra set of eyes for this. I could really use a friend and some help here." She relaxed her cocky stance and tipped her head toward the door. "You coming or what?"

He pressed his palm against his heart. "It is my duty to protect you while you quest for our people."

I take it that's a yes. "A'ight," she said. "Put on some shoes and let's get this started."

CHAPTER 12

*S**ex. What the hell was it about sex?*

Camille fumed as she marched toward the local precinct. Bad enough she had the mother of all wet dreams about Zacarias, then to have to deal with Rhys wanting to play tonsil hockey first thing in the morning? *A girl can only take so much.*

She was never a huge proponent of casual sex, but if the itch needed to be scratched, Rhys would likely be more than up to the task. God knew he'd never let her forget his interest, or his willingness to satisfy her every desire. She'd spent time with him in and out of his sensual dampening field, and in both incarnations; he was quite easy on the eye, gifted with a natural physique sure to please.

And her other would-be suitor?

She growled low to herself, forcing away any fanciful notions of a white-picket-fence future with the Grand Enforcer of the Fae Court. She knew she was being manipulated; buttons pushed, egos stroked in an effort to turn her into the newest puppet for the immortal realm.

Anger simmered beneath her skin, adding heat to the promise of another balmy day, and a drip of sweat slipped off her chin. She dashed the back of her hand across its escape path.

Rhys tugged her to a halt, as she'd almost stepped off the curb and into the direct path of a speeding car. The silver minivan honked as it rounded the corner, its driver too busy with squirming passengers to give her a second glance.

"If you perish in my care, dear Camille, that will be the end of your freedom."

She leveled an unamused stare at her current hero. "Really?" she said. "Death might actually bring its own kind of peace."

Rhys paled, swiveling his head slowly from side to side. "There, you are mistaken. If you were to die, Zacarias would have even more power over you."

Her eyebrows pulled together. "What? You mean he's a ... a necromancer?" That didn't sound right. From what she knew of the Grand Enforcer, she couldn't believe he practiced the dark, death magic said to poison everyone around them. He was arrogant and proud. But evil and full of malice? Nah, that wasn't right. That, she refused to believe. But it didn't stop her from filing away the question for later contemplation. She continued to shake her head and returned to her original path. After a couple of steps, her manners kicked in.

"Oh. Um, *merci, cher*. Thanks for the save back there." She tipped her chin over her shoulder, and her gaze flicked up to Rhys. A pleased grin had split his serious face, and she giggled in spite of herself. She held on to her crooked smile until the police station had come into view.

As they walked up to the wrought-iron fence, her stomach inched toward her heels. Something about houses of law enforcement chilled her blood. She'd never seen the Bastille during her early years in France, but stories about the atrocities committed behind those stone walls had haunted her childhood. During her long life, she'd avoided any tangles with major events that could have potentially landed her in jail. Granted, she did have an escape route at her fingertips; it's hard to be arrested for a crime when you look nothing like the perpetrator.

"Hey, Cam? Where you at?"

Cam blinked rapidly, then painted on her standard smile for the public. "Hey, *cher.*" She dug through her mind to remember his name but was saved by the patch above the left shirt pocket. "Ain't seen ya 'round lately. *Ça va?*"

Lt. James Buchanan shrugged, and a sheepish grin peeked through the bushy handlebar mustache. "Well, the wife cut off my drinking splurges. Got a kid on the way, so gotta be smarter with the money, *oui?*"

"Congrats, *ami.*" She patted him on the shoulder, keeping a professional distance.

The officer pinned her with a forlorn look. "Did you hear about Deacon?"

His reveal had saved her the trouble of finding a way to breach the topic and, sighing heavily, she joined him in the sorrowful moment. "Yeah. Happened to be walkin' by when he dropped." She mentally crossed her fingers, praying for more insights without actually having to go inside.

"Dang, *chère.* I didn't know that. Did you see anything?"

She shook her head. "Nah. Was on the other side of the street. Saw the crowd first, but then I recognized his shoes."

James grinned, whistling low. "Him and those damned spectators," he said. "Asked him about them once. Know what he said?" He stroked his walrus-worthy lip-fairy. "Said they brought him luck."

"That sounds like him fo'sure." Deacon was nothing if not superstitious. She'd once caught him rubbing a gris-gris bag he'd sworn had been made by Marie Laveau herself, before choosing lottery numbers. He didn't win, of course, but that never had stopped him from keeping his rituals. "Gonna miss him," she muttered softly.

They shared a quiet moment of mourning, and Cam tucked her hands into her pockets, contemplating how to get more information. She was aware of the silent sentinel off to her left, but since no sound of breaking glass came from behind her, things were relatively safe.

"I hate to cut this short, *chère*, but I was actually heading out," said the officer. "Seems someone else has gone and dropped dead, and no one knows why."

"What were—"

Cam elbowed Rhys in the gut, halting his interrogation attempt. "And the heat ain't even hit hard yet," she commented, hoping her diversion would redirect the lieutenant's laser focus.

James flicked his gaze behind her but shrugged off any further attention. Then he smirked, lifting one shoulder. "Gonna make for a long summer, *oui?*"

She joined him in the gallows joke, giving him a final wave as James jogged down the steps before slipping into his parked car. Her calm demeanor lasted until his silver Crown Victoria had rounded the corner; once his vehicle was out of sight, she spun about to face Rhys.

"C'mon." She grabbed his wrist and charged inside. Another sputter at her back started, and she quickly shushed it. "Don't say anything. Trust me." Determined, she walked straight up to the desk sergeant, who smiled as she approached the glassed-in station.

"Pardon, *cher*. I was lookin' for Lt. Buchanan."

"Bu—"

She drove her heel into Rhys's instep, and as his pained grunt verified her aim, she smiled patiently for a response to her inquiry.

"Sorry, *chère*. Just missed him."

Cam snapped her fingers in mock disappointment. "Dang. I got a special delivery for him. It's a gift he wanted for his wife to bless their little one. Know how long he's gonna be gone?"

The young officer shrugged apologetically. "Might be a while yet. Found a body by Washington Square and he went to check it out."

She nodded slowly. "The gift'll keep. I'll try back later today. *À bientôt, cher*." She tipped her chin, then exited the precinct. As soon as the door had clicked shut, she took off, tracking the similar path as James's cruiser. Giddy with excitement, her legs propelled her onward in her pursuit. Sadly, the anchor in her wake had a much different idea.

"Camille." Rhys pulled against her lead as she plowed on. "I do not understand why you now wish to follow your lover."

"What!" She halted for only a moment and, rolling her eyes, let go of his arm. "How the hell did you come to that conclusion? Weren't you listening when he said his wife was having a baby?" She jogged to the edge of the block and peered around the corner to discern the most direct path to her new destination. "Following him now that we know where he's going which is gonna lead us to the next body, *capiche?*"

She muttered softly, questioning Rhys's fascination with her and sex as they neared the new crime scene. Bright yellow tape had sectioned off a storefront and the square of sidewalk in front of it, separating it from the street. Ambulances and first responder vehicles funneled oncoming traffic away from the active investigation, while looky-loos perched on tiptoes behind the flimsy barricade, hoping to glimpse a macabre view of the victim. Cam wished she could forget half of the corpses she'd seen over her long life. She mourned friends and lovers with each passing generation, all claimed by time and living now within her memory.

Did her fae friends miss any mortal companions? Was there a woman who'd stolen Zacarias's heart, only to pass beyond the Veil, leaving him alone with his grief?

A mirthless laugh squeaked out of her. Right. The Grand Enforcer, caring about anyone except himself and his precious duty? Highly doubtful. Dismissing the silly notion, Cam slipped through the growing crowd and edged closer to the hustling activity. She spied Lt. Buchanan in the middle of a cluster of officers. Luckily, his attention was focused on his job and not on the ogling masses. So, with a tug on Rhys's arm, Cam dragged his head down to hers.

"How close do you need to be to the body to see if there's any, I don't know, magical stuff on it?"

A confused frown creased his forehead, and she darted her gaze around the scene, searching for a better way to explain. Waving him closer, she craned up on tiptoe, her lips a breath away from his ear.

"I need you to find out if you're sensing that same trace you felt on Deacon, on this new victim. If not, then we can leave and search elsewhere."

Realization sparkled in his amber eyes, and he motioned her forward. In silent tandem, they crept closer to the vehicular blockade, inching between the onlookers. Cam's heart hammered. Rhys was like a bull in a china shop simply walking down the street. How the hell would they make it through this throng without bringing everyone's attention to them?

Seems fate had gifted the man with some stealth, and they arrived unnoticed beside the coroner's vehicle. The white van's back doors had been flung open, the body lying inside in unobserved repose. *Not like he's going anywhere.* She bit her cheek to stifle a giggle at her own morbid sense of humor and stood guard while Rhys slunk closer. Once again, her pulse quickened. Her luck hadn't been so hot during this venture up until now. If the body turned out to be some hapless slob, then she was out of leads. Never in her life had she ever crossed her fingers for nefarious actions.

She pulled her thoughts away from the "what ifs" and focused on the "what is." Her gaze darted through the shadows until she glimpsed Rhys, who stood on the safe side of the crime tape, arm outstretched toward the panel van's gaping back. She sucked in a breathy gasp as a crime scene tech, dressed in stylish protective booties and matching latex gloves, crawled in through the passenger door. Just as quick, he slipped out, and Rhys thankfully remained undetected.

"C'mon, c'mon, c'mon," she spat out in a harsh whisper. Opting for tactics of her own, Cam closed her eyes and shifted her features. If she hadn't run into the lieutenant earlier, she could have simply been herself, nothing more than another local drawn out by the sounds of sirens. She lightened her hair color, morphed her green eyes to brown, and plumped up her cheeks a bit. With the simple transformation complete, she wove through the crowd on a different path, her focus on the bent heads of the gathered officers. They were talking details, and she needed to know what they'd discovered.

Cam edged in as close as possible and, stretching her neck until it nearly popped, took a deep breath and called on her human magicks, otherwise known as her finely honed bartender hearing skills. Intent and fixated, she grabbed up useful snippets and phrases, among which were a name, an estimated age, a gender, plus a hint at the time of death. Nothing more was known about the cause, at least until the coroner got the body back to the morgue.

"Oy! What you doin' over there, son?"

Her heart sank into her boots as every head swiveled toward the opposite side of the cordoned-off square.

Just when things seemed to be going so well.

CHAPTER 13

Rhys lifted his intent gaze from the corpse, the weight of a thousand eyes on him. Apparently, his investigation hadn't been as unobserved as he'd originally hoped. If he could only make the slightest contact, all of their questions would be answered; the trace of magic, no matter how faint, would sizzle along his fingertips. If luck was truly on his side, he might be able to determine exactly who'd cast the original spell.

If he didn't get himself caught first, that is.

"You hear me, boy?" The request had split the air once again, and Rhys searched for the perturbed speaker. A uniformed officer stood near the hood of the boxy conveyance, glaring in his direction. The man folded his arms across his portly chest, shifted his bulk from one foot to the other. "I said, get your butt behind that line."

Cautious, Rhys withdrew his arm and ducked back under the bright yellow banded barrier, and once he was again on the pedestrian side of the scene, activity resumed. Rhys shuffled back, mumbling apologies as he bumped into other onlookers, and as soon as he'd made his retreat, he scanned for his companion. To his eyes, creatures with any magical attributes emitted a glow. Humans would call it an aura, but to him and his people, it was the inner light of power. All beings radiated it, yet only those who could wield it could generate enough of a field around them to both mask and tap into the magicks. The lack of glow around Camille was a puzzlement and one he'd ask her about later. She did blend in well with the human population, though, hiding easily among them.

So easily, in fact, he was unable to identify her. The original crowd had thinned out, replaced by the newly curious. Even with his height, Rhys couldn't locate Cam's long black tresses and panic began to steal the heat from his blood as he circulated through the distracted throng. Each young woman he spun about glared at him, their surprise quickly melting into flirtatious interest. Even one man with a thick black ponytail and deep green eyes had slipped a note into Rhys's hand with a wink and a smile.

"Are you quite through partner shopping?"

Rhys swiveled his head toward the familiar though somewhat perturbed voice. Camille stood to his right, her adept fingers lacing her straight hair into an intricate plait. Relief washed over him, and he wrapped his arms around her.

"I am so grateful you were not lost," he said. His body jumped to life at the simple embrace; her soft curves enticed him, and his shaft throbbed.

She wiggled her arms between them, eased away from him. "Ain't about to get lost in my own city, *cher*." An adorable smirk tugged up one corner of her plump lips. Was she warming to him?

He leaned down, intent on capturing her mouth to test out his theory, when she arched an eyebrow up and the playful grin vanished from her face. Her expression shift paused his seduction.

"No?" he remarked, awaiting her permission to proceed.

"Are you just not used to hearing that phrase?" she said, then she sighed wearily, slipping out of his loose hold and, judging by her determined pace, had set her feet to a specific destination. "Rhys, why can't you just be my friend? Don't you have any female friends you haven't banged?"

He jogged to catch up to her. "Banged?" he asked.

"Yeah. Screwed, laid, played hide the salami with." She glanced over her shoulder as he puzzled out her strange words. "Nothing?" she said. "How about this one: fucked?"

Realization filtered in. "Ah! Made love to," he said. "Why do you have so many titles for the same act?"

She offered half a shrug. "Guess it all depends on who the partner is and if it means more than just a quickie."

"Quickie?" He frowned, scoffing at the crass descriptor.

Camille tossed back her head, laughter spilling out toward the heavens. Had he said something amusing once again? In truth, he didn't care about the "why" behind her reaction. As long as she continued to grace him with the intoxicating sound of her vocalized joy, he'd act the buffoon.

She'd mentioned friendship, and he mulled over the concept. His people were not known for their platonic relationships. Intimate, toxic, dominating, or venomous? Sure. Those were prolific, many of which had roots in some event having occurred centuries earlier. But in the area of companionship with no strings attached, his brethren lacked the compassion needed to create a bond that brought a balanced measure of happiness to both parties.

They walked along in silence, and Rhys discovered he

welcomed the peace of the simple moment. His gaze drifted to the surroundings, many of which had an air of familiarity; buildings and businesses with bold signage declaring a wide variety of products and services stood out in his recent memories. They were following the path that would return them to her abode.

"Did you learn anything, *cher?*"

He glanced around, noting the disinterest from any passersby. "Is it safe to discuss this, um, here?"

Camille chuckled, shaking her head. "Most folks don't care much what happens 'round them, unless it sounds like gossip. This is gonna sound more like crazy people talking. That gets ignored all the time."

"If that is the case"—he nodded, hastening his strides—"then I have little news to tell you. The body carried only a faint lingering of magicks. It could have been from an amulet purchased at one of the many voodoo shops in the area, but nothing that would lead me to believe it had been the cause of the person's demise."

Cam frowned, gnawing on her bottom lip as she slowed. "Well," she said, "I got some info. The woman's name was Janice Fredrickson, and she was a forty-five-year-old mother of three."

"Does the name have any meaning to you?" He was prepared to offer his condolences, and he silently prayed for any reason to once again hold her in his arms. Her apparent lack of grief, though, dashed away any hope for another physical reunion.

"Nah," she declared flatly. "Ain't one of the bar regulars, and from what I caught, she didn't live anywhere near Deacon." All too soon, the alley behind Gator Bites loomed, and as the day edged closer toward late afternoon, night, as well as Zacarias, would soon descend. Rhys clamped down on his back molars, suppressing an ungentlemanly growl.

Why did the queen trust that sorcerer of all people? *And why has Camille become so enamored of that ass?* In his realm, females of good taste and breeding avoided the Grand Enforcer, astutely leery of his rumored darker desires. Apparently, though, those qualities acted like a magnet to humans. But Rhys was a knight, and it was his duty to protect Camille, even if it was from herself and her bad judgement.

A set of running footfalls scurrying up behind them in the quiet, deserted corridor captured his attention. Their other comings and goings from Camille's home had gone unnoticed. Curious, Rhys turned to glance over his shoulder just as a balled-up fist connected with his jaw. Stars exploded into his field of vision, and he staggered back. Had someone followed them from the crime scene, or was this a random act of violence?

"What the—"

Camille's voice cut short, and he shook his head to clear away the fog. Camille was in trouble; a figure draped in a hooded jacket was corralling her into a corner. Determined, Rhys drew back his arm, only to crack his elbow against the bricks behind him. The sharp sting centered him, and he snapped his focus into the moment. Camille had ducked under a telegraphed strike, then drove her knee into the assailant's gut. A decidedly masculine grunt huffed out from the doubled-over form.

At once, Rhys dashed into the fray just as the man cocked back his arm, and in two strides he'd laced his fingers around the attacker's collar. It'd been centuries since he'd brawled, but the buried reflexes were quickly flaring back to life. With a strong yank, Rhys jerked the ruffian off his feet and flung him away. Magic danced across his skin, answering the unspoken call from his opponent, and Rhys spun about, shock mingling with anger.

"Don't stick your nose where it doesn't belong." Dangerous menace echoed in the raspy voice, and panic chilled Rhys's blood. The attacker fired a volley of punches at Rhys, driving him back into a row of trash bins, before the concealed head swiveled toward Camille, who landed a jaw-cracking blow.

"Wait!" Rhys cautioned while he prepared for a stronger counterattack. Magic would act against magic, leveling the playing field, keeping the odds in their favor. Apparently, though, Camille had a different plan.

"Wait?" Camille tossed over her shoulder as she hid behind her raised fists. "Wait for what? Him to kill me?" Her head jerked back, the force of her opponent's attack knocking her off her feet. Rhys took a step forward, sparks flowing between his fingertips as he primed his power, his attack flawless ... except for the round metal lid on the ground that caught his foot. He lost his balance, and the spell fizzled out.

"Really?" Her disappointed groan echoed through the narrow alleyway, and he stammered sheepishly while the man moved to rush past. "Stop him!" she yelled.

Angered by his repeated failures to protect Camille, Rhys tackled the fleeing assailant, driving him into the nearest wall, where the man struggled, lashing out, squirming toward the open exit.

Rhys tightened his grip on the cretin's baggy jacket, hoping a secure hold would halt any further escape attempt. Silver glinted in the long rays of the vanishing light, and he scooted back, narrowly avoiding the razor-thin blade. The sudden shift threw him off balance, and his knees buckled, pulling both men to the ground. Intent on keeping Camille safe, he called to his magicks once again but a sharp sting across the back of his hand stole his concentration. The scuffle ended with an untangling of limbs and footfalls disappearing into the growing darkness.

"Rhys? You okay there?" Camille's voice, laced with concern, encouraged him to regain his feet. She tipped her chin toward his hand and the long red welt that reached from his knuckle to his wrist. He shook his head, touched by her compassionate interest.

A slender trail of blood leaked from a cut on her lip, and he brushed his thumb against the wound, healing it without thought. Something scratched against his palm and he opened his fist to reveal a scrap of fabric. Patterns of white and black swirled on a faded red background, threads of sooty gray clinging to the captured prize.

He tipped his head toward Camille, a relieved grin touching his lips. "Now we have them by the bowls."

Camille groaned, rolling her eyes. "Balls, *cher*. By the balls. We really need to work on your human."

CHAPTER 14

Camille rubbed at her aching cheek as she climbed the rickety fire escape entry. In her present, bedraggled state, using Gator Bites' main entry beside the front doors would set off a furious firestorm of questions. Her thoughts already ran circles in her tired mind, and missing necessary sleep over the past two nights was not helping. Ever since Zacarias had darkened her bar, her life had gone into the shitter. Now, she had some maniacal delivery man stalking her.

What next? Angry pixies pissing in my coffee?

Behind her, Rhys babbled on about something, but she'd already tuned him out before she'd hit the bottom rung of the wrought iron ladder. At this moment, she only wanted two things: quiet, and a shower. Food and a serious nap followed in a close second, but after having gotten slammed into the dumpsters, she knew she smelled like the south end of a north-bound cow. Her head was pounding, and the banquet Rhys had set out for her that morning had long since been burned away. Her powers might not drain her energy as much as her fae companions' energy did theirs, but her minor dance combined with the brawl had sapped her reserves.

She stepped off the landing and onto her balcony, raising one hand to stall Rhys in the midst of his ongoing dissertation. "*Cher*," she said, "I know you mean well." Her back against the window, Cam fumbled with the latch, then swung the pane open. "I really do. But right now, I want to get inside to get a head start on cleaning up before King Asshole shows up and—"

"Well, so pleased to hear I have moved up in your eyes to rate as royalty."

Cam cringed, anger and embarrassment blending into a weird, delightful concoction, and she snapped her gaze over her shoulder to Zacarias, who lounged on her couch.

"Don't people like you need to be invited in before they can enter a house?" she snapped.

Inside, the TV created a barely audible distraction, while her traitorous cat, Alley, perched happily on the fae's lap. "That only works for vampires, dear." Guess Rhys's spell hadn't lasted long; her furry friend's coat had returned to its ebony sheen, and if not for her half-lidded bright green eyes, her cat would have been completely camouflaged by the rich matte-black of the leather pants encasing a pair of strong legs. Her intruder rested one arm across the back of her small sofa, like a ruler surveying his domain while he stroked Alley's sleek fur.

His domain? Her treacherous body yearned to dash across the floor and join the petting party, to curl itself into the open space against his side. But, no. This was her house, *her* territory, and she'd rather chew on glass than grant that man the satisfaction of knowing just how turned on she was.

Aw, shit. She clamped down on her back teeth to stifle a hungered groan and continued to wriggle into her apartment. "Well, next time, how 'bout you wait your vamp ass outside until I get home, *oui?*"

"*Pourquoi, ma minette? Je pensais que tu m'aimais mieux à l'intérieur.*"

Her native tongue had dripped from his lips like honey—rich and intoxicating—and he smiled, obviously pleased by his quadruple entendre. *He thought she liked him better inside?* He'd called her his "kitten," but the possessive phrase had a more dangerous feel; it wasn't simply a loving term of endearment.

Realization slammed into her like a fist. Her dream hadn't been just a dream; that bastard had somehow invaded her mind.

"You manipulative son of a bitch." The bitter words burned her tongue as they tumbled past her lips. Anger and betrayal swirled, shoving her earlier high-school-like adoration into the farthest corner of her heart. "Who the hell do you think you are?" Her hunger had vanished, her stomach knotting as she swallowed her roiling emotions. The smug grin on Zacarias's sensual mouth slipped and the sparkle in his electric blue eyes dimmed. Cam stared on, astonished by the unexpected appearance of regret.

"Did you not enjoy—"

Only Rhys's grand entrance as he tumbled off the window seat shocked the mood back into proper perspective. Never in her life had she been so grateful to hear breaking glass, and the thick tension shattered just as easily as the knock-off Ming vase that now lay in slivers on the floor.

Rhys climbed to his feet. "Was there a reason we came in through the—oh." Venom had poisoned his final word. Frost had slipped in with Rhys, and the previous mood returned, but with a markedly dangerous flavor. The air crackled as the two powerful fae stared daggers at one another. She should have been interested in the outcome of the impending brawl. By all rights, she really should step between them.... *I should also lay off the bourbon.*

"You know what?" she interjected, and two sets of angry eyes darted in her direction. "I'm gonna grab a shower." She plopped down on the arm of her couch and yanked off her combats. "Don't hurt my cat and clean up your own damned mess if either of you assholes break anything else."

She climbed to her feet and, not caring about their reaction to her odd declaration, marched directly into her bedroom, peeling off her shirt and tossing the smelly article of clothing over her shoulder. If she hit either of them with her sloppy shot, then it was a win in her book.

Without breaking stride, Cam stepped out of her jeans, then reached back to unlatch her bra. She paused; she had yet to close her door. Never before had she been overly prudish with her body, so why should she care about the opinions of two meddling fae boys? An evil smirk tugged at the corner of her lip and dressed in only a pair of black boy-cut undies, she dared a glance back into the living room before she slipped her arms free of the slender, shoulder strap elastics, her actions purposefully seductive and slow.

She half-expected Rhys's jaw to truly hit the floor the longer he stared after her—was he actually drooling? His counterpart, however, played it cool. Unnervingly cool. One eyebrow quirked up as he watched her spontaneous striptease with feigned disinterest.

Jerk. She turned back toward her true destination but twisted her arm behind her before letting the supportive lace drop from her fingers. Then, with all the grace of a trailer park diva, she flipped them off and stepped into the bathroom. The splashing of the water on the sides of the tile stall almost drowned out the deep, rumbling laughter that slipped under the door.

Almost.

Unsure how long her crass distraction would keep them from killing each other or ruining her chance of ever getting back her security deposit, she showered in record time. Plus, the prospect of either one opting to take her up on her offer added speed to her routine. The shower was barely big enough for her to move around in; having another player in the tub was completely out of the question. She chuckled as she recalled the last time she'd brought a guy to her place; no matter how much she tried to lead him anywhere else, he was determined to get busy in the bathroom. The bed was a more than adequate place for any and all matters of antics, and she'd even tested the four wooden corner posts to ensure they could withstand some serious flailing. Instead, her partner had preferred the phone booth of a shower stall.

His loss, she mused. After knocking his knees into the glass door, braining himself on the showerhead, and nearly losing his anal virginity to the spigot, he'd stormed out, furious and flustered, railing on her about her lack of proper facilities. She had gotten a giggle as he left, still trying to put his clothes on over his wet skin.

She hip-bumped the faucet knob, ending the tepid stream and, whistling an off-key jazz standard, Cam wrung the excess water out of her hair before a stray thought froze her fingers. In her haste to make a memorable retreat, she'd neglected to grab a change of clothes. She gnawed on her bottom lip as she contemplated her possibilities. Her invisible, sensible self perched on her shoulder and tapped her sensible shoes, smirking a "told ya so" smirk. *Bitch.*

Towels became togas, and she double secured the corner flap under her armpit. She'd have to do laundry much sooner than expected, but it was better than the alternative. So, head held high, she marched her turbaned butt out of the bathroom, pointedly ignoring the wall bisected by the exit door.

It was closed.

A curious frown pulled her eyebrows together. Chivalrous behavior? *But who?*

She continued to ponder possible answers as she rummaged through her closet. Rhys was the knight; not the same definition as she was used to, but still a Dudley Do-Right by trade, so it would make the most sense for him to be the gentleman. Yet, when her thoughts turned to Zacarias ... she wouldn't put it past him to pull this kind of dick-swinging show of power. She thought she'd caught a glimmer of an emotional response when she'd confronted him earlier, but then again, it could have been a trick of the light, or just another twist in his controlling game. After a heartbeat, she dismissed him as her potential hero. No way would that man do anything altruistic. Did he even know the meaning of the word?

A timid knock drew her out of her internal argument, and she cinched tight the drawstring on her baggy sweatpants. She punched her arms into a black, long-sleeve shirt before she padded over to the door on socked feet and swung it open. Rhys stood beyond the threshold, rigid and tense, and she tugged down the hem of the shirt while she peeked around him, searching for signs of a struggle.

"We did no damage to your home." His jovial tone had vanished, replaced by an unaccustomed weight to his voice. Cam chalked it up to being cooped up with Zacarias during her quick sluice.

She painted on a sympathetic smile as she sidled past. "*Merci, cher*. I do appreciate it." Zacarias had moved from his throne on her sofa to holding up the wall near the kitchen, and neither looked particularly pleased to be in the same space. Cam rolled her eyes and shook her head, saddened by their childish behaviors.

As she headed across the living room, she mentally admonished herself, though. She knew nothing of the history between the two of them. Bad blood definitely flowed, though the exact cause of the rift was unknown to her. They were ancient beyond her imaginings, and she was well versed in the pettiness of her fae brethren. Her mother had told her of family feuds that had lasted for centuries because someone had placed yellow flowers instead of orange blooms at the table. Yet, the visceral current that flowed through her confining apartment spoke of something more serious than a mere decorative goof, and if she didn't break the strain soon, her meager belongings might end up as casualties in the impending battle.

"Did you find anything out about the logo?" She opted on a neutral topic and finger-combed her damp hair as she made her way to the kitchen table where her laptop sat idle; a lone silver rectangle on the round blonde wood.

"Well..." Rhys hedged, and Cam cocked up an eyebrow, glancing his direction.

"Please don't tell me you broke my computer," she said, irritation bleeding through her words. She just had the damned thing refurbished a month ago after some drunken asshole at the bar had spilled half a hurricane on it.

Serves me right for thinking it'd be safe under the bar. Dismissing her panic, she flipped open the cover, and to her relief,

Elvis sneered at her, his perfectly coiffed black hair hanging across his forehead.

"I told you we needed to open it somehow," Rhys crowed proudly. Cam shifted her gaze as the lanky fae created his own personal victory dance, an adorable smile splitting his face while he gyrated awkwardly. She chuckled at his celebration, although the scoff at her back told her just what Zacarias thought of the display.

"Congratulations," he enunciated, his sneer evident in his caustic tone. "Too bad your idea of where to lift would have more than likely shattered the device."

Why did he have to be such a jerk?

"It's not brain surgery," she added, upping the snark level. "It's just a laptop."

Silence coated the room.

Dammit. She dropped her shoulders, immediately regretting her cutting words, and her head hung heavy off her neck. She sighed. "That was rude," she said. "I'm sorry. I'm just really tired, and I'd like to get this sorted out soon so my life can get back to normal."

Zacarias grumbled as he sauntered out of earshot, but she could have sworn she'd heard him say: *You're not the only one.* She fired up her device, refusing to give him the satisfaction of her response, fingers hovering over the keys as her gaze scanned the bare table.

"Uh, Rhys? Do you still have the patch?"

She ducked her head to search the floor beneath her chair, then patted her non-existent pockets. Her eyes narrowed as she struggled to recall anything about the design. "Black with red? No. There was—"

An oval scrap of fabric appeared in her periphery, the hand holding it shaking ever so slightly. She frowned, glanced up at Rhys. "You okay there, *cher*? You look a little green."

His golden skin had a chartreuse sheen, and his tawny brown eyes were missing their spark. He gave a weary shake of his head, accompanied by an equally weak smile. "I am fine," he replied.

She *tsk*ed him, then set her attention back to her search. "Well, if you decide to take a trip out of denial," she said, "there's more Cokes in the fridge. The sugar might help you feel better." She drummed her fingers on the table, pondering the hows of finding the design's origin. Because the bulk of the logo was white on pale red with a ring of black, she feared the low-quality camera would only capture a pink blob ringed in grainy charcoal.

"What are you attempting to do?"

Cam swallowed back her intended response to Mr. Asshole and continued to stare at the pictures whirring past on the screen. "We grabbed a patch off the guy that jumped us in the alley. Now I'm—"

"Jumped you?" A chilling edge to Zacarias's voice drew her eyes away from her computer. Sparks flashed in the depths of his own electric blue ones, the odd glow comforting. "You were attacked?"

A cautious grin tugged at the corner of her lips, and she dipped her chin. "S'all good, *cher*. The guy seemed more driven to give us a good scare than anything else."

Zacarias remained scarily still, holding her gaze—Was he worried about her, or was he afraid she might fail in her task?—while her own conflicted emotions struggled to illuminate the tense silence. But, realizing nothing would come of this staring contest, she instead pointed down to the embroidered scrap. Zacarias followed her movement, and Cam heaved a relieved sigh.

"Uh, Rhys snatched this off of the guy's jumpsuit, and we need to figure out what it means."

She lowered her gaze back to the screen, grateful to be out of the Grand Enforcer's direct, penetrating stare, and scrolled through image after image, frowning at the sea of squiggly lines and strange patterns. Her eyes darted between her laptop and the smug little swath of fabric. At first, the design appeared to be a stylized capital Z, but the swirls and curlicues made it less like a single letter and more of a glyph; an amalgam of several things layered together to create something unique.

A warm presence crowded in over her shoulder. "May I?" She peered behind her, a worried frown sweeping away her smile. Rhys swayed unsteadily, sweat replacing the shimmer that usually coated his face.

"As long as you sit down before you fall down," she said, and she yanked out the chair next to her, then reached up and captured his sleeve. It only took a light tug for him to collapse beside her. "Are you really sure you're okay?"

"Perhaps I have gone too long away from my home."

Cam frowned. "Never heard of homesickness actually being, well, a sickness." She shifted the angle of her computer to share the screen with Rhys.

"The energies found in our world are, shall we say, different from those in your realm," Zacarias chimed in, and he stepped in to hover between her and Rhys. Cam leaned away from his cloying presence and swiveled about to lock eyes with him. She sat quietly, waiting for him to explain more. "The fae have specific needs that cannot be met in the mortal world." He paused, locking his unearthly eyes with Cam's before continuing. "Or by mere humans."

His derogatory tone irked her, and she slung her arm across the back of her chair. "What, other than food, water, sleep and, well, things like that?"

Why couldn't she say sex? She was no blushing virgin, but even thinking the word with him so near seemed dangerous. Honestly, she didn't know what she feared more: his taking the mention of sex as an invitation, or that she'd want him to.

"Yes, child. Other than those."

Aaaand the asshole returns. She clamped down on her molars, but not quick enough. "Ain't no child, *cher.* And I'd appreciate if you'd stop calling me that."

"If you knew anything about your mother, you'd know she needed to replenish her magic from time to time." Piercing electric blue eyes pinned her with a bored stare. "Have you no memories of her leaving you?"

"Only at the end." Anger overrode her civility, and unbidden tears blurred the scene before her. She could have sworn his perfect mask slipped once again, though it might have been her wavering vision or perhaps a desperate imagination. Had she glimpsed another fleeting moment of empathy, the lines around his inhuman eyes softening? Her chin quivered at his unexpected response though she refused to be swayed by the temporary lack of cruelty in his handsome face.

"She wasn't like any of you," she explained. "She was, and I am ... different."

Snippets of remembered conversations with her parents bobbed and rose over her flood of conflicting emotions, and she sifted through the words and wisdoms her mother had passed on to her. In her mind, a field of wild daffodils unfolded. She'd chased the early spring butterflies flitting between the bright yellow blooms, while her parents had strolled hand in hand behind her.

She loved Marseilles in April. The soft rains would bring blankets of color to the hills, spilling down into Vieux-Port. Long before she'd learned about the monsters and the many faces they wore, she'd learned about her roots and the unique magic she'd inherited.

"Are there others like me, maman?"

Laughter like the tinkle of bells filled the air. "*Non, ma chère. We are the last of our kind.*"

"Doesn't that make you sad?" She'd celebrated only twelve birthdays, and to her young mind, life was either happy or sad. Her parents had done their best to keep the happy times more numerous than the sad; she'd watched the families in their little village laugh and celebrate, generations gathered together in joy and in sorrow.

Her mother ruffled her ringlets, her warm smile shining brighter than the sun. "Sad? *Pourquoi, ma petite?* How could I ever be sad with you and your papa to keep me company?"

The topic of her heritage would not be breached again until after they'd arrived in the New World, and she never once remembered any days without her mother by her side during all those long years.

Shoving the memories far away from probing minds, she jumped to her feet and snapped her gaze to the silent sentinels standing beside the table.

"Why don't both of you just go back to fairy land then? If anything new pops up, I'll send a message." The segue was harsh and jarring, but she wanted to make it clear the previous topic was officially closed. Rhys glanced away and made a beeline toward the kitchen, but the Grand Enforcer held his pose.

With her feet firmly planted on the ground and the carpet acting as her "line in the sand," Cam glared at Zacarias, daring him to make the first move. She locked her jaw, struggled to dismiss the clatter of dishes against tile over her right shoulder, yet it was the heavy thud that followed that finally grabbed her attention. She jerked her gaze away.

A pair of overly long legs now poked out from behind the cabinets, and she rushed over to Rhys who lay sprawled on the cold tile, dish shards surrounding his head. She searched the floor. Was there a puddle, or even an uneven seam to explain his fall? *How could someone so ethereal and magical be such a clod?*

"Come on, Grace. Let's get you off this..."

She touched clammy skin, heat nearly singeing her fingertips, and her throat locked. "Zacarias!"

"Has the oaf knocked himself unconscious?"

"Dammit, get over here. Something's wrong." Cam had thrown her angered words over her shoulder, not caring about her tone. She was done with Zacarias and his elitist crap. Right now, as troublesome as Rhys was, he was a friend who needed her help.

CHAPTER 15

"By the gods, what now?" Zacarias muttered as he stalked away from his vantage point near her bedroom. He'd spent most of the day dividing his time between checking on his ailing queen and her daughter, and struggling to dismiss the lingering emotions from his dreamwalk. Originally, he'd intended to take Camille on his terms and slake his immediate need; she was naught but a pawn chosen by Tannequil and slated with an impossible task. Why not take what he wanted and be done with her?

Even now, his mouth watered in memory of her sensual responses. She was a willing partner, receptive and eager throughout his seduction. Was that what stopped him from plundering her body with no remorse?

"I ... I don't know." Her stammer had yanked him from his musing and encouraged him to pick up his pace. "He's burning hot to the touch," she said.

Zacarias rounded the narrow kitchen island and dropped

down to her side. While Rhys was no friend, he was still one of his kind. A thin sheen of sweat glimmered on his skin, dulling his natural luster, and in the air hung a faint tinge of a sickening sweetness, the odor a blend of stagnant waters and rotting winter wheat. Zacarias recoiled, raising a hand to shield his nose, while at his feet, Rhys's eyes fluttered weakly, as though the effort to lift the flimsy lids was too much to bear.

"I am sorry," Rhys slurred, breath rattling, while his gangly limbs slipped across the white linoleum. "I must have eaten something which did not agree with me."

Cam shook her head, her thick braid easily cutting through the miasma. "I tried to warn you about eating too many fried oysters. Just take it easy there." With almost tender care, she ducked beneath his arm and guided Rhys over to the couch. Envy crawled along the back of Zacarias's neck, and he sneered at her sympathetic expression.

"If you are quite through playing nursemaid," he said, his irritation sharpening the edges of each word, "perhaps we can get back to the task at hand." And he gestured over to the shiny computer screen before folding his arms across his chest. Did he care he was acting childish? Not particularly. Rhys interfered with his royal duties. And his personal agenda.

Camille shooed him away with a flippant wave. "Cool your jets, *couillon*. I'll be right over."

He narrowed his eyes, though he was more irked by the brush of her fingertips across the man's forehead than her actual words. He cared naught about intruding upon their intimate moment. She was a tool for *his* queen, not her conniving sister.

Seconds ticked by, and she rose to her feet. Concern had crinkled the corners of her crystalline jade eyes, and her playful smile was sadly absent. Zacarias scoffed. How could she feel anything for the oaf other than a host's pity for a sick guest? So why he now offered her the comfort of an embrace, he'd never know.

"In general, we are difficult to kill," he whispered gently as he held her close. "But some elements in the human realm do not mix with our physiology."

"Like alcohol?" Her head snapped up, and she darted her gaze back to the couch before meeting his once again. He nodded. Her features relaxed, and she shook her head, forestalling any further discussion.

"Some places do add beer to the batter. That must be it." Her expression shifted; stern lines hardened her soft lips, and her jaw clenched. "Guess it's gonna be just you and me working for a while."

She wriggled out of his arms and plopped down into her chair to resume her furious search. Images and pictures flew by as she tapped angrily at the innocent device, and Zacarias looked away, the sea of rolling patterns threatening to make him ill. How could she keep any of those flashes straight in her head? He picked up the physical evidence, opting for a slower path, sensing a lingering trace of dark magic, ancient and powerful, still clinging to the threads. Something familiar lay in the painful sparks climbing up his arm from the light contact.

"Don't move it," she groused, grabbing one end of the cloth. A primordial jolt shot between their joined fingers, and she released her hold on it.

"Are you sure that is the way the design is meant to be viewed?" He tipped the image onto its side and leaned away to gain perspective. "It seems you have been looking at it wrong."

She frowned up at him, massaging her hand. "Wrong? What do you mean wrong?"

He stepped up close to her back, wrapping his arms to either side of her to hold the design in front of both of them. "You have been searching for this pattern," he remarked, steadying the patch on a vertical plane. "When we should be thinking of it"—he tilted the squiggly lines and leveled out the center line to create a completely new configuration—"this way," he said.

"Now this one I've seen." Her breathy voice sent blood firing below his belt line. Gravity, and a force with an even stronger pull, dragged his chest closer to her body. Yet, for each inch he neared, she slouched ever closer in her scrutiny. The dance had only lasted a heartbeat before she lurched back, nearly knocking him from his feet, and he staggered to regain his balance and dignity, while she muttered a rapid apology then scrolled through the images once again.

"Where was it ... where was it ..." she mumbled to the dizzying blur of symbols, and his eyes lost focus until the world before him locked into place.

"Stop," he barked out. "Go back."

She did not rebuke his command; instead, she rewound the images, pausing before moving on to the next. The long-forgotten symbol popped into view, and he gripped her shoulder.

"Damn."

Camille glanced up from her screen to pin him with a determined stare. "Something you'd like to share with the rest of the class?" she said, echoing his own words from their initial meeting.

Up-tilted, her face shone in the artificial glow of the modern technology. Yet, nothing could diminish her ethereal beauty, her plump lips ripe for kissing. Inches separated them. All he had to do was fall forward and—

"That," said Rhys, "is an ancient death curse."

Zacarias swallowed a death curse of his own as the knight thrust himself into their conversation. Her angelic face vanished, instead giving him the top of her head. *Well, that view might be just as good.* Dismissing the crass thought, he refocused his anger toward the appropriate target. Rhys's coloring was still pale, and his aura now pulsated with grays and flashes of deep umbers.

"Death curse?" Camille swung her gaze from Rhys, to her computer screen, to the patch, and then up to Zacarias. After her second dizzying circuit, Zacarias moved to stand at her opposite shoulder. His chivalrous gesture did put him within arm's reach of the thorn in his side, yes, but he would suffer a fool to take the smallest burden off her plate.

"Not exactly a curse like you are thinking," Rhys soothed. The strange odor from earlier had continued to grow, as if emanating from Rhys, and the man scratched incessantly, itching at the back of his hidden hand with an odd determination. "It is a bastardization of a Greek symbol for harm."

Camille tilted her head, shifted her gaze back to the screen. "Harm?" she said. "Sounds a lot like a curse to me. Maybe not voodoo, but some powerful gris-gris to be sure. So, does harm mean anything, or anyone, specific?"

Zacarias contemplated the wheels that spun inside her intelligent mind—she viewed problems from many angles and analyzed several possible solutions. He reconsidered his original, and rather limited, appraisal of her. Perhaps she was smarter than he'd first assumed, and the additional measure of her quick wit ticked more points in her plus column. If he wasn't careful, he might end up admiring her for more than her erection-worthy ass.

"It is rather open for interpretation," Zacarias tossed out, offhandedly. "However, it is generally reserved for curses more personal in nature."

A deep furrow cut across Camille's forehead, and she tapped her chin thoughtfully. "So this is someone who has an axe to grind with someone in your world. Fabulous. Well, that might cut down on the number of possible suspects." She paused. "Just how many people have you guys pissed off over the years?"

"How much time do you have?" he responded in a droll tone. "Our kind has not been known for our, shall we say, compassionate natures." The myths and legends surrounding the mischievous behaviors and antics of the fae did not happen by accident. Many nights, he'd taken part in the plundering of hapless humans who'd wandered too close to the Veil separating their worlds. The simple-minded were so easy to manipulate, and he, as well as his brethren, were always in need of entertainment. Eternity could be so boring.

"And as I am sure you have noticed," he continued, "this part of the country is quite the hub for supernatural beings."

Her soft laughter wrapped around his shaft like a velvet glove. "Y'ain't kidding on that one there, *cher*." Damn, but that woman was sensual without thought or action. "I guess that's why I always found my way back here over the years," she said. "Just made me feel..."

Her voice drifted into silence. With a concerned frown, he shifted his gaze and caught the panic in her eyes an instant before she bolted out of the chair.

"What ha—"

Her frantic gestures froze his tongue as she scrambled to

grab the TV remote, and he sat back on his heels as she increased the volume. Something had captured her undivided attention. Curious, he stepped closer to the droning newscaster in mid-story.

"...dragged a body from Lake Ponchatrain today. There were signs of a struggle, indicating the possibility of foul play. Police are questioning area residents, but as of now, they have no suspects."

On the screen, an odd scene played out with officers in deep blue uniforms covering the discovered corpse with a yellow sheet. Then the picture shrunk, relegated to a small box in the upper right-hand corner, while another reporter's face dominated the camera. Their informational conversation continued, but Zacarias had already lost interest; instead, he was much more curious about Camille's excited response. She pointed toward the TV, bouncing on the balls of her feet.

"That was him. That was him."

"Him, who?" Zacarias frowned at his weird, owlish inquiry.

Camille rushed back to the table, snatched up the patch and held it aloft like a beacon. "Him, him! The guy who jumped us. I recognized the boots and the overalls before the police covered them up." She shook her head fervently. "I know what you're going to say, but I tell you: It was the same guy. They must have taken him out when he failed to kill me. Or us, I should say. This has to be the piece that connects all the deaths."

"But who are they?" Rhys had stumbled in once again, with the obvious question of the hour. An unusual, breathy weakness sat in his voice, one that betrayed a sinister start. Zacarias shifted his narrowed eyes toward the knight errant. *So this is how the illness begins.* The degrading aura, the scent of decay. All of it, Zacarias had seen before, but never in its infancy. Rhys was still in control of his faculties. *For the moment.* Only time would be the judge of how much longer he remained so.

"Work."

Camille's whispered word had cut through the silence. Zacarias turned away from the walking dead man to focus on her. "Come again?"

She stared a moment longer at the swath of fabric she held before swiveling her face toward him. "Work," she repeated. "That has to be it. I remember seeing this design on a keycard in Deacon's wallet. He'd flash it when he was fishing out money. I never paid much mind to it before." She paced around the narrow confines, eyes focusing on the ground as she made circuitous paths. "And that woman they found this morning. She had a lanyard with it all over it, on top of her belongings."

He followed her rhythmic gait with his eyes, drinking in the shift of her hips with each step. Beneath the blousy fabric, muscles clenched and released, bunched and then lengthened, as she strode past him, unaware of his scrutiny. The leather encasing his legs was a poor substitute for the heat of her sheath, and the longer he stared after her, the more blood rushed into his cock.

She halted, then dashed back to the computer. Another flash of inspiration?

"I don't know why I didn't think of this earlier," she mumbled. He peered over her shoulder as her fingers flew across the letters. He'd caught the words *New Orleans business logos* at the top of the still image before it vanished.

"What are you hoping to find?" he asked.

The screen winked on once again. Beneath the top banner stood an array of small pictograms in neat, organized rows. In the center sat the object of their search.

Camille spun about, grinning proudly as she gestured to her discovery, and his own lips tugged up, joining in her well-deserved celebration. The complete collapse of Rhys onto the floor marred the moment, however, and one of his hands slipped from beneath the blanket wrapped around him to reveal a toxic web of blackened veins spiraling out from a red and angry gash.

"If you know where this business is located," Zacarias stated, "I suggest we waste no time." She paused in her efforts to pick up the unconscious knight, panic tarnishing her beauty. "Rhys is infected."

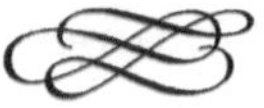

CHAPTER 16

Camille tapped her fingers against the steering wheel. She wasn't worried about her driving skills. It had been a minute since she'd taken her '92 Volkswagen Jetta out of the garage, but some talents didn't fade. In truth, who cares if she totaled the beater around the next curve? Her thoughts were focused on her ailing friend now trapped in her apartment.

She gnashed her teeth. Rhys and his stupid lie. Food poisoning. She should've known better. At first, she'd thought he'd been seriously injured during their minor skirmish and had been afraid to admit it. He was male, and a knight to boot, so getting his ass kicked by some hoodie wearing punk might not do well for his street cred. But this was different. A shudder crept along her skin as she remembered the trails of brackish green spider webbing spreading out from the hairline scratch on the back of his hand. Not even an hour had passed and he was steadily declining.

"The light has changed."

"Huh? What?" The words had crept into the cool evening

silence, reminding her she was not alone in the car. *What did he say?* She slid her gaze over to the passenger seat, where Zacarias leveled a bored stare at her and pointed to the traffic signal.

Muttering a combination thanks and apology, she stepped on the gas and headed toward the city's outskirts.

"Are you certain you are going the correct—"

"Would you quit asking that?" she said. "If you know a quicker route to Westwego, then you take the damned wheel." She'd long-since stopped counting how many times he asked his version of "are we there yet?" after pulling out of the driveway. "Patience ain't one of your virtues, is it?"

Did he have any virtues at all? Vices, he had in spades. He was decadence wrapped in a silken glove, which wouldn't be so bad, except he knew it and reveled in it.

The temperature inside the cramped cabin climbed upward as his hand caressed her knee. "I can take my time when needed," he purred.

She squeaked and flinched, her knee jerking up into the dash. "If you want to have this talk now, that's fine by me." Self-preservation had kicked into gear, and she yanked the wheel toward the sidewalk. Tires bumped into the curb before the car came to a sudden halt. Her seat belt became a shield, keeping her safely on her side of the interior. "You stole into my mind and invaded my dreams," she said. "I don't know much about where you come from, but here, that's seriously crossing the line."

His confident smirk faltered. *Good.* She forged ahead. "Even if I thought you were good looking, when I said no one in my room, I meant it. Your people might not put much stock in trust and honesty, but I do." She'd risked one finger jab in his direction before pointing to her own chest. "I am going to find this cure only to help my friend, got it?"

She turned away and shoved the car back into drive. "As soon as Rhys is cured, I want you all gone. I like my simple life, and I'd like to get back to it as soon as I can."

"Do you?" His soft voice had still managed to fill the empty space. The scenery whizzing past in the setting sun altered the farther they drove away from the city proper. Buildings dwindled in size and number, shifting from single-family dwellings to sprawling warehouses. The smell wafted up from the Mississippi River and squeezed in between the closed vents. Cam was grateful for the thick, lingering aroma; its unique odor dampened the heady cologne Zacarias must have bathed in.

Her brain fumbled for a response. "Do I what?" Why couldn't she focus for long enough to answer his damned questions?

The silent seconds ticked by beneath the whir of her engine. She drew her eyebrows together, glanced sidelong at her quiet companion. The heat from his gaze was strangely absent, yet his electric blue orbs bored into her very soul.

"Do you truly wish to return things to the way they were?" he asked.

She pulled her attention back to the road to ponder her reply. What did she have that was so amazing she hungered to get back to? She had a decent job; tending bar might not have been the most noble of all of her career paths, but she enjoyed it. From behind the thick oaken barrier, she watched the world go by, with no one the wiser to her mixed heritage.

The introduction of her distant relations into her day-to-day dealings had turned her routine upside down. Nothing was normal anymore. Each minute brought new and unexpected adventures. Plus, she had two men. No—scratch that. She had two drop-dead gorgeous beings built for sex and promising nothing but pleasure, vying for her.

For me.

Did she really want things to go back?

Before she could respond, a gleaming structure of glass-and-chrome came into view just on the other side of the canal, towering above the decrepit derelicts along the warehouse district, its garish neon sign's meaning now so obvious. Zacarias was right. She had been looking at the design going the wrong way. That ancient Greek symbol was emblazoned across the entryway like a badge of honor, yet instead of reclining across the door frame, the image stood straight and tall, proud of its cryptic warning.

Zonular Tangential Biotech Industries. Residents called it an eye sore. Employees called it Zon-Tan.

"Bio-tech?"

She nodded, navigating the sharp turn guiding them to the bridge. "Short for biological technologies," she replied. "It means they make medicines and do medical research."

He grabbed onto her shifting hand, his death grip in jeopardy of cutting off all circulation. "S-s-s-stop."

Panic shot through her veins, and she stomped on the brake. She tried to pry his clenched fist from her aching hand. "What's wrong?" she asked, the words tumbling out in a frantic rush. "What happened?" Her knuckles cracked and groaned as she struggled to slip free her fingers and, praying for answers, she bit her lip, shifted her gaze to Zacarias. Pain had contorted his handsome features—muscles popped out along his jaw, and his steely gossamer glamour shimmered and cracked, its ethereal glow shifting and dimming. He banged the back of his head against the raised rest.

Was he having a seizure? Did immortals have epilepsy?

"G-g-g-go back-ck-ck," he hissed out. Cam bobbed her head rapidly and threw the car into reverse. She jerked around and kept her eyes on the road behind her bumper, while she wrapped a comforting arm around his shoulders, and after a few tense moments rolling halfway up the block, he let out a relieved huff.

She yanked on the parking brake, then unlatched both of their seat belts. She patted him down, unsure of what she was doing, or even what she was looking for. She slapped her hands against his chest and squeezed his upper arms.

"Are you okay? Are you hurt? Do I need to call for help or something?" His rapid breathing gradually calmed, and he captured her trembling fingers. Her gaze climbed up to his face. The tension, as well as his shielding glamour, had vanished, and Cam gasped, taken aback by his unaltered beauty. Skin the color of starlight and exotic, up-tilted almond eyes were framed by platinum blond locks. Long, thick lashes like butterfly wings painted dark crescents across the tops of his chiseled cheeks.

In his vulnerable state, defenses down, he was beyond exquisite. This was a face that inspired lust-filled fantasies and the willingness to die for one more kiss. His lips parted, and she watched in rapt fascination. A crease had appeared above his still-shut eyes, and once again, his mouth moved.

"I am fine now." Fatigue lingered in his voice, and Cam had the overwhelming urge to lay her head against his chest. It wasn't sexual. Not completely. But she did want to comfort him. Wanted it more than she dared to admit. And she wanted to hold on to this tender moment for as long as possible.

"*Ta sûr, cher?*" she asked. "What was that, anyway?" She waited, giving him time to answer. He gave her hands a reassuring squeeze before releasing her trapped fingers, and she almost spoke up. Instead, she nodded and crawled back to her side of the car.

Once she was safely behind the wheel, Zacarias transformed to his human-safe version. Just as it was for Rhys, the glamour only muted his perfection to a tolerable level. She thought of Rhys's unearthly eyes. Would the blue be somehow richer without the dimming power of magic?

"I believe that was a bulwark." He re-secured his seat belt, as though to dismiss the entire subject. When the silence deepened, he glanced sidelong at her. "Oh. My apologies. A blockade of sorts. Think of it like a shield. It stops my kind from entering into certain places."

She nodded as her brain churned. "But it didn't affect me," she remarked.

Zacarias answered with a half-hearted shrug. "It must be due to your mixed blood." Strange ... it didn't sound like an insult when he said it that time. Either she was getting used to his churlish nature, or he was paying her his version of a compliment. "Regardless," he added, "I believe we have found the correct location."

"Can't argue with that," she agreed. "So, let me guess: I'm on my own."

His sinister smile sent chills along her skin; mirth didn't sparkle in the electric blue depths. "You could just let him die and we could fuck in the front seat until Armageddon arrives." And just like that: in place of the earlier angel sat the asshole.

Cam tossed her hands skyward, knocking her knuckles against the low-hanging roof. "Are you kidding me? That's where your mind went?"

He arched one eyebrow and, resplendent in all his dickish glory, he peered at her from beneath heavy lids. "Tell me you don't find the notion even somewhat intriguing."

Up until about two seconds ago. She huffed and reached across him. If he thought she'd warmed to his suggestion, he was in for an unpleasant surprise. With a swift pull, she yanked on the passenger door handle and flung the door wide. And as she returned to her seat, she clicked open his safety belt's fastener.

"Out." She revved the engine, making her answer crystal clear. "I'll pick you up on the way back."

His laughter had filled the cab long after she'd torn across the gravel on the side of the road, and he was still laughing as he faded into the distance of her rearview mirror.

What a jerk. What the hell was I even thinking?

"You were thinking with your heart; a trait that will get you killed in my world."

Cam growled at the invisible voice. "Note taken, *cher*. Ain't gonna make the same mistake again." She shifted gears, her car easily passing through their earlier roadblock. Nothing. Not even a tingle, like walking across a grave.

"Be on your guard. Their alarms might have been triggered by my attempts to cross the threshold."

She parked her car far enough away from the main doors for her quickly concocted story to work. "Don't tell me you really care if anything happens to me?"

"Would it be that difficult for you to believe?"

"Honestly? Yes." She tossed her phone into her trunk, then

locked things up tight. "Now shoo. Let me be and get out of my head."

A warm caress from an impossible source brushed softly against her cheek. *"Do not take any undo risks."* The moment passed, and she was again alone. Had she misjudged him?

CHAPTER 17

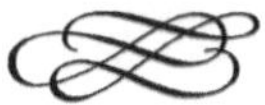

The sun had set into the hills by the time Camille had reached the far edge of the parking lot. A handful of cars sat scattered in the massive open space, though it was clear the office was closed for the day. Fingers crossed, she painted on her best "damsel in distress" expression and headed straight for the entrance, feeling the weight of hidden eyes watching her every move. Cameras peeked out from under eaves and were proudly displayed on high posts lining the path that led her ever onward. She spied a solitary guard sitting behind layers of glass and a chest-high wall of desk. The chrome barrier revealed only his head, but she was certain a bank of security monitors held his attention.

She grabbed the door handle and gave it a tug. Much to her surprise, it opened easily. Crap. Maybe they were still open.

Why would that bother her? Hell, she didn't even know what she was looking for. Maybe a giant flashing arrow pointing down a hallway saying: "This way to the secret lab!" Grumbling at her naïve appraisal, she forged ahead.

A clean-cut young man glanced up from his hidden duties. "Can I help you, miss?"

Miss? Definitely not a Southern boy. No man raised below the Mason-Dixon Line referred to a woman of any age as "miss." She couldn't place his accent, but his features smacked more Mediterranean to her—olive skin, black hair and eyes, and a haughty Roman nose, all visible trademarks. She heaved a false sigh of relief, then stepped up to the desk.

"Oh, *cher*, I sure hope so." She smiled, laying on the charm as thick as molasses. "See, my car got a flat back there, about a half-mile. Are you the only one working here now? Could use a hand to help me change it out."

He blinked, unmoved by her performance. "Sorry," he said. "We're closed."

"*Merde*," she muttered, loud enough for him to overhear. Meanwhile, her mind spun. What if Zacarias was right, what if they were waiting for her to screw up so they could jump her? "Would I be able to use your phone so I can call for a tow?"

"Don't you have a cell?"

Was that a tiny crack in the armor, a hint of curious concern?

She gnawed on her bottom lip, shook her head. "I do, but I left it at work." Another chink appeared, and she lunged at the opening. "Please, *cher*. It won't take but a minute."

He watched her warily for another second, then nodded and reached beneath the counter. He set out an archaic, corded phone. "Just dial nine for an outside line, miss."

"*Merci beaucoup, mon ami*. Thank you." She repeated her thanks as she dialed her cell. The phone rang, and she smiled, nodding. After an appropriate amount of time, she began her act anew and, speaking rapidly in pigeon French, she visually surveyed the scene, feigning a balance of tired frustration and nonchalance. The guard eventually lost interest and returned to his seat.

Free to look in earnest, Camille catalogued important details for later. A set of thick steel doors behind the guard hid the bulk of the building, while brochures stood at attention in wire racks placed near all possible entryways, with a couple of informational trifold flyers and a business card holder filled with generics within easy reach. Nothing too helpful, until she spied a pair of free-standing signs: *"Welcome Donors"* topped a distinguished column of names. She recognized many of the wealthiest families of the Gulf Coast, mixed with corporate tycoons. *Luck must be smiling down at me,* she thought. The exclusive event was slated for tomorrow morning, something that no doubt included a tour of the entire facility. Assured the ruse was complete, she wrapped up her fake call.

"Merci, Antoine. A bientôt, cher." She set the receiver back into its cradle and stood on her tiptoes to deliver the phone to him. "You are a godsend. Mind if I take one of these?" She motioned to the pamphlets as he took the phone from her.

"Help yourself."

She smiled and grabbed one of each. "Thanks again, *cher. Au revoir.*" Camille tucked the papers into her back pocket, waved, and walked out the door. Behind her, she recognized the audible click of a walkie-talkie and she strained her ears to listen as she continued calmly toward the exit.

"Negative, sir. Just a local with a flat tire."

She forced her breathing to remain steady and stepped outside. No alarms, but that didn't mean she was out of danger.

Before the door clicked shut, she caught the tail end of the one-sided conversation.

"Correct, sir. Her aura reads human. Must have been another glitch."

Sending a silent prayer of thanks to her father's strong genes, she crossed the parking lot, retracing her steps back to her vehicle. Any doubts about the status of Zon-Tan had been smashed with the guard's parting words, and once she'd reached the halfway mark across the open pavement, the eyes boring into the back of her head shifted away to surveil the empty lot.

Now, for the really hard part. She pondered as the lights behind grew fainter. *How the hell am I gonna get in there to get what Rhys needs?*

She stumbled over a stray rock in the darkness as the truth of her question hit her. Funny, Zacarias had given that original order. But he only *wanted* it; Rhys *needed* it. She began to imagine the cure like a tangible object; a gemstone or a reliquary. Something physical and, more importantly, something in limited supply.

Once she'd crested the last berm, she noticed a beat-up red pickup parked close behind her little sedan. Out from around the truck's snub nose stepped an older gentleman, his dingy overalls grease-stained and well-worn. She jogged the final distance, waving and calling out to get his attention.

"Sorry, *cher*. Had to make a nature stop." Good enough excuse for leaving a vehicle. Heaven knew these long roads along the riverbanks didn't have built-in rest stops.

The old man smiled and nodded. "Know the feeling, myself. Just wanted to make sure no one was hurt out here or something."

Talk about timing. If any interested parties were still following her movements, she couldn't have asked for a more perfect alibi. She engaged the man in polite conversation, focusing on the workings of cars, specifically how to change a tire. He was more than knowledgeable, walking her through the entire procedure from start to finish. She wished she could have requested the *Reader's Digest* version of his lengthy description of the many varieties of lug nuts, but she needed him to stay for a reasonable amount of time.

She smiled, thanking him profusely while climbing into the front seat and closed out the night, just as the first drops of rain splattered on the dusty ground. Once safe inside the sanctity of her car, she gunned the motor and headed back along the river road. She'd abandoned Zacarias nearly an hour ago. Would he still be laughing when she picked him up? Would he still even be there?

"Probably hitched a ride with a sex-crazed bachelorette party."

"Sadly, no."

Cam let out an embarrassing squeal as Zacarias materialized in her passenger seat. She jerked the wheel, nearly tossing the car into the dark waters below as her hand flew up to her chest, determined to keep her thumping heart behind her rib cage.

"*Bon Dieu*! You trying to scare me to death?" She mumbled obscenities in every language she could think of while gathering her scattered wits. A few deep breaths later, she returned both hands to the wheel, but not before giving him a good thump on the arm for her troubles. "Didn't your maman ever tell you it's rude to sneak up on people?"

He heaved a bored sigh. "We've already had this conversation. And no, to answer your early inquiry, I am not attempting to frighten you into an early demise. What did you learn?"

The New Orleans lights crept steadily closer, appearing and

disappearing with each swipe of her windshield wipers. "That's definitely the place. Whatever they're doing there, they're keeping it under a tight watch."

"Did you see any others?" He leaned in, his breath tickling her cheek. An absent excitement had colored his words, but she wasn't eager to placate him. Plus, she herself hadn't truly processed all she'd gathered.

She lifted one shoulder as she maneuvered her car through the light foot traffic. Only the most torrential downpours kept people off the streets of the Big Easy. "Just a guard at a desk. A couple cars were still in the lot when I got there, but they were gone by the time I left."

Zacarias opened his mouth to begin another round of twenty questions, but she raised a hand to stall any further interrogation. "*Cher*, can't tell you what I don't know." She rolled to a stop in her parking spot four blocks from her apartment, then cranked up the emergency brake. "Let's just get you inside and work it out from there, *oui*?"

She cringed inwardly, knowing her flippant words could be so easily twisted by the overtly sensual being, and heat marched up from the rolled neckline of her white tank top, stopping only when it was buried deep beyond her hairline. She fumbled with the seat belt latch, then crawled ungracefully out of the car's cab, refusing to glance his direction. By the time Zacarias had uncurled his limbs and exited the vehicle, she was soaked.

Great, drowned rat. Always such an enticing look. Angry at herself for even caring about her appearance, she patted the roof after locking up her car and, certain things were secure, Cam picked up the pace, eager to get out of the rain and to gain some needed distance from Zacarias.

Raucous music pouring from the open windows of Gator Bites grew louder the closer they got to her apartment, the lively zydeco rhythms blending with hoots and hollers from the energized patrons. Never before had she wished so much to be back behind the bar; she envied her old, boring life and longed to return to the days when she was the only freak in the room. Curiosity had finally gotten the better of her as a stray thought ran through her mind.

"Why were you still there?" She'd seen him vanish into thin air. He could have gone anywhere, but instead, he'd joined her in almost the exact same spot where she'd dumped his ass.

An umbrella appeared, shielding her from further damp. She kept her hands tucked under her armpits, not only because it was warm, but also because it was safe.

"I wanted to be sure you made it out alive." His answer was clinical, almost rehearsed in its delivery.

She scoffed and shoved open the door to the main stairwell. "Hope you didn't hurt yourself with the outpouring of emotions there. Oh, that's right. I'm a valuable tool. Can't let the tool get damaged."

"No, I..."

The rapid, unguarded words drew her to a halt and she cautiously snapped her gaze up past the arm holding the umbrella. His haughty demeanor wavered, and he dropped his shoulders a noticeable fraction.

"I did want to make sure you were okay," he said. She detected a hint of open honesty, mixed with a pinch of compassion. The rare kindness had wiped away the harsh lines around his full lips. Yet part of her screamed out in warning. He was the Grand Enforcer of the Fae High Court, loyal to beings known for their manipulation and treachery. At this moment, she was of value to them, but who knew what the next second would bring?

Opting to give him the benefit of the doubt, she offered him a crooked but guarded smile. "*Merci, cher.* But what could you have done if I weren't? Not like you could've strolled in to save the day, *oui?*"

An ominous shadow fell across his face, and any trace of his earlier compassion was burned away in the cold fires in his unearthly eyes. "There are more doors than those that are visible."

Cam shuddered, blaming the damp night for the chills crawling along her arms. She hastily climbed up the stairs, propelled forward by her urge to check on her friend and by the tingles slipping down her spine. His terrifying, cryptic words called to mind Rhys's earlier accusations.

She'd denied Zacarias to be a dealer in death magic. Now, she was not so sure.

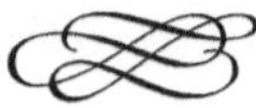

Pain ebbed and flowed, dragging Rhys in and out of sleep. After discovering their big clue, his heart had filled with pride and with purpose. True, he did need to brush up on his battling spells; it had been so long since he'd witnessed actual combat, and he'd always preferred the healing arts. He called forth the image of Camille grappling with the unknown assailant, proving herself to be quite capable of handling almost anything.

The tiny scratch across the back of his hand had seemed nothing more than a minor wound; an itch only skin deep. Once inside her small dwelling, though, the burning had spread—prickling heat had burrowed into his muscles, stealing his strength. When he awoke on the floor with Camille aiding him to regain his footing, he'd been truly embarrassed. It was his duty to help her, not the other way around.

He'd fought against the growing discomfort until it had

surpassed his tolerable threshold. Only the harsh words of the Grand Enforcer had cut through his mind's dizzying fog.

"He is infected."

Rhys did not fear death; it was nothing more than a concept to be suffered by others. He had no real knowledge of what passing beyond the Veil would involve, much less the notion of taking the journey himself. Yet here he was, thrashing about on a narrow couch, wrapped in a thin blanket that offered warmth even as it stole it from his body.

He clamped his teeth shut, lest he cry out again. Time had no sense of flowing. He was trapped in unending agony and he only wished for a small reprieve. In his fevered state, he'd heard voices calling to him. Many he did not recognize, their words unclear, but their basic messages were like spears piercing his soul.

Strip him of his title, they whispered. *How dare you call yourself a knight if you have done no noble deeds?*

Wave upon wave, they heaped on the hateful sentiments. He pictured the face of Lady Maeve, his mistress. Her ruby-and-gold spun locks barely shifted as she shook her head, disappointment and pessimistic disgust stamped on her ageless features and her sapphire eyes betrayed neither grief nor despair at his passing.

It was foolish of me to send you on such an important task. Now all our people will pay for your failure.

His body rocked, and Camille took her place, her turbulent and rich green orbs so near, he nearly believed them to be real. A deep furrow creased her pale forehead, and her full pink lips pulled down into a frown.

"You still with us?"

Had his tormentors found a new way to make him suffer? Her

voice cut through the invisible speakers, and another set of tremors shot through him.

He blinked rapidly, then forced his eyes to open, only to discover they already were. This was no hallucination. "You are here?" he said. Camille had returned. She knelt by his side, a cautious smile drawing up the corners of her mouth.

"Well, I do kinda live here."

He slithered beneath the clingy blanket, scooting into a more seated position, and her hands guided his shoulders to the cushioned back, her light touch both soothing and searing.

"Ain't gonna bother asking how you feel, since you look like crap, *cher*. No offense."

"None taken." He chuckled weakly. "I can assure you I probably look better than I feel." If this was going to be his end, he did not want her to worry for him. Instead, he took the chivalrous path. "Were you successful in your searching?" he asked.

She heaved a burdensome sigh, then perched on the edge of the table. "Yeah, on some level." She shifted her gaze over his shoulder. As if on cue, a new set of footfalls announced the approach of the third in their party. Zacarias appeared in his periphery and chose to sit in the open chair at the foot of the sofa. Rhys wanted to glare at the man, but the petty reaction required more effort than he was willing to waste.

With everyone gathered, Camille pulled a handful of papers from out of her back pocket. "Zon-Tan is definitely the culprit," she said. "They had a 'You shall not pass' shield for your kind surrounding the place and—"

"You were alone among dangerous enemies?" Rhys fought to sit up straighter, prepared to give Zacarias a piece of his mind, but Camille smiled and patted his shoulder gently.

"You wouldn't have been able to get through it either. And besides"—her demeanor shifted—"they were on alert, expecting some sort of trouble."

"The alarms were tripped," Zacarias said, though the statement was more self-directed rather than open for discussion.

Camille glanced up and nodded. "*Oui.* They got security upon security upon security there. I didn't get a good look at their system, but I heard the guard say as I was leaving that my aura was human."

"Aura? They can detect and determine species' auras?" Rhys shook his head, trying to wrap his fevered mind around the magicks needed for this.

"I would guess so," she admitted. "That doesn't mean other, well, races can't get in. Who knows, maybe they employ supernatural creatures? Maybe the keycards allow them to get past the gate?" She tossed the gathered materials onto the table as she jumped to her feet. "Hell, I don't know. Maybe I'm just making shit up and I'm running out of ideas."

One of the folded sheets fell open to reveal colorful images of smiling people in pristine white coats. A female face grinned at him from across the distant past. "Zacarias?" he said, his voice no more than a whisper. He called out again, pointing to the solitary figure on the page. He had to get the Grand Enforcer's attention before darkness and pain pulled him under.

Zacarias rolled his eyes, then leveled his perturbed gaze. But as the man's cerulean blue orbs followed the line of Rhys's extended arm, his countenance changed as realization flooded over him, and he nodded. The standard sneer had vanished, giving Rhys a brief glimpse behind the arrogance.

Rhys smiled at the tiny sign of respect, then succumbed to the abyss once more.

ZACARIAS WAITED until Rhys had slipped back into unconsciousness before he signaled to Camille. He would not take credit for the knight's discovery, but the news he had would be delivered best without him listening.

"Camille?" he said.

Why was he whispering? He glanced toward the bundled figure on the couch. Rhys wouldn't be waking up any time soon. *If ever.* Camille remained still, her back to the room as she stood by the window overlooking the cityscape.

"Camille?" he called out again, louder and more confident. She jolted, lifting a hand to wipe her cheeks. *Was she crying?* Confused and curious, he crossed the room to stand behind her. He hesitated, his arm reaching out to her. Time was now an enemy; if they wasted too much of it on sappy emotions, more than one life would be lost.

Armed with this driving knowledge, he placed a comforting hand on her shoulder, then gently turned her about to face him. She sniffed and swallowed hard, her gaze fixed on the floor.

"I'm tired of watching friends die, Z." He arched a brow at her abbreviation but did not correct her. Instead, he hoped his silence would encourage her to work through her emotional roadblock. "I've seen my share of death—necessary, accidental, sometimes even deserved." She dropped her head back to gaze up at him with heartfelt grief. "How do you deal with an eternity of this?"

A single tear had clung to her lower lashes, and he brushed

away the stray drop with his thumb. "Life has a different meaning when you realize there is an end to it." An adorable frown had tugged her eyebrows together, and he offered her a soft smile in lieu of a more physical form of reassurance. In truth, standing this close, his body warred against his conscience as he hungered to savor her lips outside of the dream realm. He tipped his head back to the room. "Come," he said. "We may have found who's behind this."

She nodded sharply, any additional peeks of feminine weakness shored up behind the familiar iron wall. "Okay," she said, stepping out of his reach, and his spirit mourned for the loss. "Was there something helpful in the promos?"

While she moved away from him, he growled, readjusting his swollen cock. "Hard to believe, but yes."

"You okay there?"

I'd be more okay buried balls-deep inside you. He silenced his rampaging thoughts and limped to the table. A quick visual check on the blankets showed movement. Rhys wasn't dead yet. He leaned down, gathered up the colorful brochure, and pointed to one smiling figure.

"This is her. She is the one behind all of this."

Camille screwed up her face, swung her pendulum gaze from the professional image to him and then back again. "Her? She's ... she's a doctor. A leading researcher, according to this, and—"

"And an aerico who once loved the queen's consort." He folded his arms across his chest.

"Ooh ..." She'd drawn out the single syllable with a long breath. "A jilted lover. But what's a ... a ... whatever you said before."

"An aerico is a Greek demon of disease. Vicious bitches who

thrive on misery and suffering. Most of the folklore surrounding them describes them as tiny creatures living off the sick and multiplying like rabbits." He shrugged. "Let's just say that some things let people only see what they want to have seen."

Camille's head bobbed up and down as he spoke. She took the pages from his hand to continue her study. Soon, the furrow across her brow made a repeat appearance, accompanied by a sad head shake.

"So she creates this virus that can wipe out immortals, and what? Does a test run on humans?" Camille set the pages back onto the low table. "Hang on a sec. Won't that kill her man? I mean, is she that angry that she wouldn't want him back?"

Zacarias sneered at the idea. "Back? Why would Lord Baltazar want her, after spending any time with Tannequil?"

She chuckled, tsking his logical response. "You're clearly thinking from his perspective. He might never take her back, but that doesn't mean she won't still try."

She had a point there. He tapped his chin as he rethought his stance. "Perhaps that is true. Women have been known to do strange things when they're in love."

"Speaking from experience there, *cher*?" Her teasing tone hid an edge of curiosity, and Zacarias shifted his gaze, only to see her scurry out of the living room. Was she hiding from him?

"Only from what I have seen, *ma minette*," he replied in a slightly raised voice to ensure it followed her into the kitchen. The rough and somewhat unladylike groan from the other room told him his rejoinder hit his intended target and he grinned, pleased.

"But this means she probably created an antidote, as well." Glasses clinked and rattled, and a thick door whooshed shut before she emerged with a pair of green bottles, the same as the drinks they'd shared the previous night. Again, she easily removed the tops with a flick of her ring, then handed him the beverage. "It makes sense, *oui*? That way, if he got sick, she could use the cure as some sort of bargaining chip."

As she took a long pull from the bottle, he observed her carefully, watching her throat muscles ripple as swallow after swallow passed her lips. His cock ached, jealous of the green glass. Seconds ticked by, and his eyebrows tugged together while tears slipped down her cheeks, and the contents had nearly been drained when he reached out a hand to stop her. She coughed to regain her breath, yet he was unsure whether she was choking on the beer or on her sadness. He set their bottles down onto the table and rubbed broad circles against her back.

"There has to be a cure," she said. "There just does." She turned her forlorn gaze up to him. "What are you guys doing with all the sick people where you are?"

He sighed, recalling the deathlike sleep of his queen and her daughter. "In the hopes that a cure does indeed exist, we have placed those infected in a *dormir congelat*. It's like a forced hibernation. I believe your scientists refer to it as 'suspended animation.' It is halting the progression of the disease. For how long, though, we cannot say."

Camille perked up, a spark returning to her soulful eyes. "Then you can take him back there and pop him in the freezer with the others, *oui*? Right?"

He held no previous love for the meddling knight, but now his opinion sank even lower, dragged down by his own jealous envy of Camille's apparent blind adoration. Had the buffoon bungled his way into her heart? The longer he chewed on this thought, though, reviewing all the interactions involving all three of them, the more he realized he was overreacting. She was kind, and her kindness extended in many directions. Friends. He could allow a friendship with another man, but nothing more.

Armed with his rationalization, he turned his gaze back to her creamy emerald pools. She hungered for good news from him, and he wished he could give it to her. She deserved the truth, no matter the pain. He took a deep breath to steel his nerves, then held on to her shoulders to offer compassionate support.

"Because he is already carrying the disease," he explained, "it will be impossible for him to cross the Veil." After the first bitter pill had slid past his lips, the color drained from her cheeks and her chin quivered, anticipating the final nail.

"I am sorry, Camille," he said, then paused and forced out the words that would break her heart, "but he must be saved in the human realm, or he will die in it."

CHAPTER 19

Camille sat on her bed, knees tucked under her chin as she stared out at nothing in particular. Zacarias's warning of doom and gloom played on an endless loop in her mind, refusing to give her rest. Here, or nowhere. The only choices Rhys had. Did immortal creatures have heavens or hells? Where did their souls go afterwards?

Or were souls only given to mortals?

Too many theological questions added into the frenzy of thought, and she dashed the back of her hand across her leaking eyes again. She'd told Zacarias she was tired of seeing friends die. The truth had hit her deeper than she wanted to admit. Rhys had wormed his way into her heart and had become a friend. She'd found his innocence and inherent kindness refreshing. Even if he was trying to get her between the sheets, never once did he shirk from his promise to keep her safe.

She hugged her legs close to drive away the shudders and to banish the visions of his current fevered state. There had to be a cure. She wouldn't let any other possibility seep into her thoughts. Her rationalization for the existence of an antidote were sound; any sane person would create a way to reverse the effect if the wrong people were caught in the crossfire.

And if it's real, it's behind those thick doors.

A soft knock roused her from her musings. Rhys was too weak to get off the couch, and no way would Zacarias be so polite as to knock on the door. She sniffed back the remnants of her useless tears and cleared her throat. A welcoming response clung on her tongue before her brain altered the reply.

"Uh, give me a sec," she said. "I'll be right out." Zacarias might have dropped the snark last night, but part of her still warned about trusting him with access to her bedroom. She climbed off the bed and slipped into the light robe hanging on the back of her door. She'd paraded around in less as a tease; now, serious boundaries needed to be set to save the friggin' world. Huffing out a heavy sigh, she opened the door, where a steaming cup of fresh coffee rested on a small matching dish, waiting for her in Zacarias's palm. Curious, she tugged her brows together.

"Where did you find the saucer?"

The corners of his full lips pulled up in a teasing, sensual smirk. "Good morning to you, as well." Her cheeks warmed, and she blamed the sudden blush on her current state of exhaustion. He dialed down the charm as she took the offered mug. "Did you sleep?" he asked.

The fragrant vapors cleared away some of the fog in her head. She lifted a shoulder, then took a fortifying sip before engaging her mouth. "Enough," she replied. Over the lip of the cup, she eyed her silent server. Dishwater blond hair fell in casual waves, curtaining the right side of his face. Yet there was no hiding from the piercing electric blue eyes peeking through the thick strands. His intent gaze spoke more than his slow nod. He took a step back, giving her space to sidle past. The silken button-down hung off his shoulders, leaving his chest bared and tempting.

Until she spied the bundle on her couch, lying too still for comfort. Then panic kicked her in the gut as the seizure hit. Rhys writhed beneath the thin blanket, head tossing from side to side, and he bucked violently as a strangled cry tore from his lips. The lights in the whole house flickered, and one bulb exploded in the nearby lamp.

Camille squeaked, the saucer slipping from her fingers as she ducked the flying glass. The small dish bounced harmlessly onto the rug and rolled for shelter under the coffee table. Luckily for everyone, the spasms didn't last long, and Rhys soon returned to his deathlike slumber. Her breath caught as she fought back the swell of tears. Zacarias placed a comforting hand at the small of her back.

"He lives still," he whispered. She sensed an upcoming "but" and waved off any more explanation.

"Yeah, I know." She didn't care if she sounded like a frog who had been gargling with razor blades. In her gut, she knew the rest, and she did not want to hear it spoken aloud. She set down her coffee and knelt down to retrieve the saucer, using the time to sort through her thoughts. Swallowing past the twisted knot of emotions, she took to her feet and turned her watery gaze back to Zacarias. "I have an idea."

The harebrained concept had first begun to stir when she looked at the photos in the brochure last night. People, standard random people, all dressed in bright white lab coats. All she needed to do was to get through those huge doors. Inside, she'd make her way into the research lab…

"…and magically find the exact room where they store the antidote and walk right out the front door."

Cam groaned, angered by two glaring facts: First, Zacarias had once again invaded her mind. Second, the asshole was absolutely right. "I didn't say it was the best idea ever; I just said I had an idea."

She kept her eyes on the shivering figure beneath the thin blue blanket. "And I don't want to hear about how it's not going to work, how it's doom to fail. I … I just have to do something."

"And you could think of no other plan than to waltz in, ask for the antidote, and bat your eyelashes as you strolled back out the front door?"

His overt sarcasm jumpstarted a new train of thought. One dangerous, yet strangely plausible. "Not my eyelashes." She cast a glance over her shoulder at her brooding companion, the pull of a mischievous smile tugging the corners of her lips up. "My pocket book."

"Come again?" He rocked back on his heels, folded his arms across his chest.

She spun about and gripped onto his biceps, the wheels in her head whirring at a dizzying speed with the burgeoning brainchild that grew and morphed into a faint glimmer of hope. "We buy it," she said, "or at least promise to fund it. Oh my God! I can't believe I didn't think of that earlier."

Her optimism buoyed her steps as she retrieved her cooling mug. "They're a biotech firm. That means they do research, and research always needs money. Always. The more, the better." She paused long enough to chug down the rest of the perfectly sweetened go-juice. Savoring the last mouthful, she pondered how he knew exactly how she liked her coffee and gave Zacarias a mental point in his favor. If she survived this, she'd tally the scores and determine who had a chance at a date. "When I was looking around the lobby," she went on, "they had these fancy signs getting ready for a donor event and—"

"Donor?"

She swung her gaze about, bit down on the inside of her cheek to hide an untimed laugh. Confusion did not look right on Zacarias; he regarded her under a furrowed brow, burly arms folded across his chest. She scooped up the flyers from the table and presented them as evidence. "Donors are people who have too much money and decide to give away large amounts of it to popular causes so they can feel better about themselves," she explained.

A chilling spark flickered in his perplexed eyes as he accepted the papers. "There is no altruistic rationale behind the gift?"

"Only if it gives them a break on their taxes," she scoffed. "Hell, I don't think most companies even care where the money comes from, as long as it's enough to keep them afloat. If I can just get beyond the front doors by posing as one of those potential donors, we might have a shot at finding the antidote."

He tilted his head, leveled his cerulean gaze at her. "We?"

She gave a quick nod, then ducked back into her bedroom. "I've got a good idea how to make it into their research facilities, but I don't know much about ancient Greek runes or any other languages they might be using," she yelled, hoping her voice carried from the closet into the living room. "I'll need you to translate any of the old stuff I don't understand." She'd need more of a business suit for this dance; hangers scraped and jingled as she shifted through her selections. *Red is too bold. Black, too somber. Maybe blue?*

She grabbed a crisp Navy blue jacket and matching skirt. Her tank would make a poor substitute for a silk blouse, but beggars couldn't be choosers. As she scanned her shoe options, she noticed an extra pair of bare feet on the carpeted floor and, making short work of the long journey to his handsome face, Cam put on her best petulant glare.

His smoldering, yet concerned look took her aback. "Just how do you expect me to help, when I cannot cross the barrier?"

She should have yelled at him for coming in without her permission. In fact, she would do exactly that, just as soon as she stopped ogling his ripped chest. Her gaze eagerly explored the bared flesh presented before her. God, he was gorgeous, moving far beyond handsome, headed straight for panty-dropping in a flash.

My friend is dying. The direct thought immediately doused any flickering embers in her imagination. She swallowed past the knot in her throat, reengaging her voice.

"We'll be going high tech for this one." She shimmied past him, ignoring the warmth of his skin as she escaped into the safety of her bathroom. "I'll have you in my ear"—she paused, pointing her chin toward her bedside nightstand before she closed the door —"and I have a pair of glasses that will allow you to see what I see."

Get dressed. Go into the lion's den. Save Rhys. She repeated the mantra while stepping into the deep blue pencil skirt. *Did I shave my legs? Do I need to?* Luckily for her, women's business fashion hadn't progressed much since the 70s. All she did was put in shoulder pads in the 80s, only to take them out again in the

90s. She slid up the zipper tab and rejoined Zacarias in the bedroom.

"Wait. Glasses that I can see through? I'll be in your ear?" he sputtered at her back as she shrugged into the slightly outdated blazer.

Holding the only sensible pumps she owned, she padded over to her nightstand, where a quick rummaging through the single drawer turned up the sleek black case. She had the idea to purchase the camera glasses and Bluetooth radio receiver after a series of strong-arm robberies had plagued various shops in their ward. Leo, one of the bouncers, suggested she wear them during shifts, and it sounded like a good plan. Even their bookkeeper, Lil Rob had sprung for the top-of-the-line model for the earbud. It was easy enough to slip the earpiece in, and her long hair hid the tiny receiver. The glasses were tricky, though, the original, overly thick earpieces a dead giveaway to the concealed spy tech. Not to mention the wacky lenses tended to give her splitting migraines. Thank God she'd found a better pair online after only a couple of months.

Brandishing the two innocuous devices with a proud grin, Cam winked at Zacarias. "State of the art. The frames have both a built-in camera and a pretty clear microphone. It's all connected through my computer, so all you'll need to do is sit back and watch the screen."

Zacarias poked tentatively at the black, horn-rimmed spectacles. "This is astonishing," he murmured. The rare awe brought a sly smile to her face. *So he can be impressed. Good to know.* After a short study, he glanced up to her. "Are you certain they will not detect it?"

She flipped his hand over and placed the items in his massive palm. "They're not magic, *cher*. It's technology." Once certain he wasn't going to break them, Cam gave him a tender push out into the living room and shut the door behind him.

She turned toward the decorative wall mirror. With her clothes on, she had more control over her dance; fabric would only give so much. Plus the restraints limited her imagination. Frowning at herself, she reached over and grabbed the colorful brochure off the small end table. Stock models were generic enough to fool nearly everyone, and it did give her an air of notoriety—people would stop and point, asking her if she was famous, since she seemed so familiar, which made her cover stories that much easier for Joe Q. Public to buy her various facades.

Rhys had asked her about her original form. Now, as she stared at her reflection, she contemplated her response. Over the past two centuries, she'd taken on so many faces and forms—old and young, every ethnicity, every size. Her eyelids drooped as she pulled up a memory of her mother. Raven hair and eyes like sparkling sapphires, she smiled at Cam from across the void. Her father's gift were her green eyes, not to mention her razor-sharp wit. Chuckling to herself, she was flooded by images of times long ago—her parents smiling as they walked hand in hand through the lush gardens in France. She hugged herself, missing their arms offering her comfort. From the rough crossing to reach the New World to the last days of both of their lives, she had spent her younger years safe in their loving shadow.

"Camille?"

Zacarias's curious tone through the closed door drew her back from her past, and she opened her eyes. Damp trails shimmered on her sun-kissed cheeks as she stared into the face of her next persona: average looks, average hair color and length. Distinguished, yet simultaneously forgettable. Perfect cover for a research investor. Certain the dance would pass muster, she sniffed back her tears and stepped out into the front room.

Makeup would need to be light but still present. She grabbed her bag off the floor and rummaged through it for her emergency go-kit. Mascara, lip gloss, and a hair tie or two were never far from her reach.

Silence filled the room, though she pointedly ignored the lack of conversation. She sensed a nearby presence and she looked away from her beautifications to glance up at Zacarias. He moved in behind her, close enough to feel the warmth of his bare skin through the blazer. All she needed was a moment of weakness and one step backwards.

Neither would appear any time soon. She gathered her stray emotions and lifted her chin a fraction.

"Zacarias," she said, "I need you to believe this will work. I don't care how crazy or far-fetched it may sound. Besides," she continued, turning to face him, "you guys tracked me down to do your detective work, and right now, this is the best plan I can think of."

She squirmed under his intense scrutiny, but an anguished groan from the couch steeled her resolve. She extended her hand, palm up. Seconds ticked by while she waited for him to answer her unvoiced request. He arched an arrogant eyebrow, and a hint of a smirk tugged at the corners of his lips.

Ugh. Men. She balled her fist and planted it onto her cocked hip. "C'mon, now. Ain't got all day. Hand over the toys." Again she beckoned, pointing to the tech still sitting in his palm, and his luscious mouth curled into a wicked grin, his brain obviously going to some misinterpreted sexual innuendo. Glancing over his shoulder at the clock on the wall, she did a quick computation: If she left in the next few minutes, she'd arrive in time for the facilities tour. But first she'd have to get her tools away from a temptingly frisky fae.

"If you want to please your queen, I'll need to get going soon," she said. The low blow hit its mark in spades, and the earlier light in his electric blue eyes vanished. Gone was the playful charmer, and in his place stood the Grand Enforcer in all his menace and fury. He rose to his full height and handed over the contents. She hated knowing her words had caused the darkening of his mood, but she was on a schedule.

If I make it through this, I'll apologize. Cam strode over to the kitchen table and fired up the laptop. A couple taps on the keys, and the screen reflected the polished wood floor beneath her feet. She swung her arm, scanning the room with nauseating results then, satisfied, she slipped on the glasses and tucked the small receiver into her ear, adjusting her hair to hide the evidence.

"Say something." She needed to make sure the batteries were still good. A test run should do the trick.

"The outfit is not extremely flattering," he said. She paused, confused by his random fashion advice. "Or is there a—"

"No." She raised her hand, pointed to the laptop. "Say something into the mic on the computer. I need to check my earpiece."

Zacarias grumbled but begrudgingly went to the kitchen table. She felt a twinge of guilt for peeing in his Wheaties, so she opted for an olive branch, crossing to stand behind his chair. As she leaned over his shoulder, his wild and heady fragrance wafted up, rich and intoxicating. She fought against the urge to curl up into his inviting lap and forget the world, intrigued more than she wanted to admit. *I'm nothing more than a tool for the fae court.* But was that truly his fault?

Turmoil twisted her gut. Great. Now, of all times, her soft, feminine side decided to make a grand appearance. She set her jaw, fingers tightening into determined fists to remain focused. Zacarias would have a chance to plead his case when she returned. *If I return.* An involuntary shudder slipped down her spine and she dismissed the maudlin thought.

"Just talk into that little ... wait." She jogged over to the roll top desk. "I've got something better." A hasty search of the junk drawer turned up the sought-after item. Her laptop was designed for gaming and came with all the gadgets and toys every nerd could desire. Personally, she never saw the lure of pretending to be someone else; she was well acquainted with that harsh reality and opted to remain out of the virtual realms, but she'd held on to the extra tech, just in case.

Armed with the wireless headset, she dropped it down in front of Zacarias, then edged between him and the computer. "Just need to reinstall the app and get it configured to..." Her verbal train of thought had digressed into mumbles while she synced all the devices, tapping and scrolling with fervor. The ticking clock on the wall encouraged her to keep her mind focused on her task and ignore Zacarias's bare chest pressing against her jacket. A huff of warm breath tickled her neck, and she scurried out of his reach.

"All you have to do is hook this over your ear and talk into the mic." She handed him the small set, then vacated his personal space, using shoe retrieval as her cover story. A small touch of makeup was still needed to complete the look, but she could finish that detail while she waited for her car to warm up. *The glasses will hide enough of my face.* After grabbing her laptop shoulder bag from the back of the bedroom door, she gave herself a final once-over then geared up.

She quickly made her way back to their makeshift operation's base, the image on the computer screen spinning and whirling around as it followed her focus around the room. Certain the earbud was safely hidden behind her upswept hair, she steeled her spine and turned to face her unenthusiastic partner.

Zacarias glowered, unconvinced, and fiddled with the small headset. "How can—"

"Dammit, Z. I don't... We don't have time for you to be doubting this. I need you to trust me. Just put that on and talk into it." She fidgeted, deciding on the best stance to get her wish. Instead of striking a power pose, she opted on a different strategy, adding, "Please."

Seemed the magic word still held some sway in the fae realm. After leveling a perturbed glare, he acquiesced and slipped the device onto his ear, while she basked in the glow of the simple victory and reached for the door handle.

"How do I look?" She painted on her best, professional smile as she stood at the threshold.

"If I were you, I'd wear a better color," he said, and she frowned, puzzled by his strange non sequitur. "You might be spending eternity in that ghastly blazer."

CHAPTER 20

The door closed, leaving Zacarias alone. A rattling breath from the couch, however, had him amending this earlier sentiment. *Well, I'll be alone soon enough.*

Camille had been correct when she reminded him of his queen's need. He'd stayed too long in the mortal realm, and now their *laissez-faire* attitude was beginning to rub off on him. He had a duty to perform and he could not allow his desired flirtations with a beauty to sidetrack him.

"Zacarias?"

Confused, he glanced around the room. Rhys still lay in his near-death sleep, and the voice definitely belonged to Camille. He swung his gaze to the small screen, where the wallpapered hallway just outside the front door slipped by and a downward stairway appeared in the images.

"Camille?"

"Well, at least everything works. Is the video working?"

He pulled the chair forward and tumbled into the wooden

seat. "How is any of this possible? Is this what passes for magic in the human world?" Fascinated, he touched the framed glass. Small shadows appeared where his fingers had contacted the pliant material but did not affect the view. He slid his hand around the edge, then looked around the back of the open metal machine.

"I suppose it could be seen as magic, but like I said, it's only technology." Transfixed, he stared on, watching the world through her eyes. *"It just took us a while to get to this point."* She slipped behind the wheel of her car, then turned the slotted key. Boisterous and discordant music blared out and he reached to his ear, prepared to yank the contraption away from his head. Before he was able to remove it, though, the volume dropped down.

"Desole, cher. Forgot to turn down the stereo."

He grumbled under his breath as the vehicle pulled out into traffic. Had her apology even been genuine?

All this new high-tech gadgetry was overwhelming. In his world, magic gave him unlimited power and control, so to find himself at the whims of a petulant little skin dancer more concerned with the fate of just one hapless fae was discomforting.

"You do know there is an easier way for me to be, ah, inside your head," he said, deftly omitting the other place he'd like to be inside.

He felt ridiculous saying the words aloud, but he was certain his one-way conversation was not being monitored. He stared at the screen as the image wiggled rapidly from side to side.

"Uh-uh. Can't take that chance." Scenery shifted and buildings melted away into open space. She was back on the path from their trek last night. *"Once I get past the guards, I can get a better look at their security setup."*

Bored by the monotonous landscape, Zacarias took to his feet and headed into the kitchen. The fresh pot of coffee was still warm, and he helped himself to a large cup. Mortals didn't get much right, but they did strike true when they'd created this delightful beverage. Granted, the flavor of the blend in Camille's home was weaker than he preferred, but he'd make do. Easy for him to ascertain her exact preference. The dark, set-in lines on the glass carafe stopped at a specific point, and stains on the small basket holding the grounds spoke of precise measurements, as well.

His brows tugged together, and he rested his hip against the cabinetry. Why had he taken so much effort to ensure the morning brew was to her liking? Did ... did he want to please her? He scoffed at the foolish notion. No, he was simply being a considerate house guest, and after her assistance last night, it was the proper response. Not to mention, he did enjoy the alluring lights that danced in her eyes when she smiled.

"Do you have much experience with gauging corporate security systems?" he asked. She'd told him the microphone attached to his earpiece would allow him to move about and still communicate with her.

A playful chuckle bled through the background noise. *"Probably a good sight better than you,* cher.*"* She glanced up from the road and he caught her gaze in the small mirror set high on the vehicle's glass shield. She winked; the edges of her eyes crinkled as she grinned, and the scene returned to the street.

He tipped his chin at her clever retort, smirking in delight. She was enchanting. At every turn, she'd proven herself resourceful, intelligent, and level-headed. And while he sensed her passions ran deeper, she managed to keep a tight leash on her emotions.

As he recalled the vulnerability, however, that had slipped

between the cracks in her armor last night, his smile faltered. Mortality was a heavy burden for her to bear. If she chose, she could have easily returned to her mother's people and been welcomed with open arms. As soon as this endeavor was complete, he'd speak to her again on the matter.

For now, he'd aid her in any way possible. Perhaps his assistance would sway her into his arms.

"Hang tight."

He pushed away from the counter, jolted out of his daydream. "What has happened?" A glance at the computer showed nothing of interest.

"Just coming to the spot where you spazzed out and—"

"I did not 'spaz out.' I—"

She shushed him with a sharp lift of her hand, and his jaw clamped shut. He stewed in silence. *Spaz out.* While he did not know exactly what that meant, syntax alone told him it was not complimentary. A light rain splattered against the windscreen, covering the scene in a thin blanket of gray.

"Anything, cher?"

He frowned at no one. "Anything what?"

She sighed, her relief washing over him, even from a distance. *"Thank God. Just had to make sure you didn't get picked up."*

She was concerned ... about him? Puzzled and pleased, he relaxed and sank back into the chair. "It seems your plan is working."

A hollow knocking echoed through his ear. *"Don't jinx it. We're not out of the woods yet."*

"True," he acquiesced. "But at least we know their barrier did not detect my presence."

The car turned onto a long and winding road off the highway

and in the distance, he spied the gleaming chrome facade shown on the front of the glossy brochure. As she approached the building, a milky haze coated the entire structure, and in his enhanced vision, he saw pulsing ochres and sparks of sickly greens oozing across every surface.

"Be careful, little one," he cautioned, leaning in closer as though able to touch the web miles away from him. "There are dark and dangerous magicks protecting things, both inside and out."

She slowed the vehicle as she neared a small shack. *"Great. Now you tell me,"* she muttered between clenched teeth. Again, her gaze darted to the mirror, allowing him to see her face. This time, her eyes showed none of their earlier mirth.

The scene shifted and she rolled down her window to address the uniformed woman with a small clipboard.

"You here for the benefit tour?"

The female face bounced up and down in his vision, yet nothing could mask the true shape of the creature.

"What does she look like to you?" he whispered, unsure how far his voice traveled from her inset device. He blinked to ensure the demonic visage would remain, and it did. The creature sneered, tusked teeth protruding from a cruel mouth as it pointed a hooked finger toward the building.

"Not now." Camille had sung the short phrase softly through a false grin before loudly thanking the guard. The vehicle started up again and followed the indicated pathway. A soft humming buzzed, then the interior was silent once more. *"She looked like Satan pretending to be a thirty-something girl in a standard rent-a-cop uniform."* Images swam as she swung the car into an open stall. *"Remember, I can see them, too."*

Oh.

All noises vanished, and she snapped her gaze to the mirror. *"Now, just so people don't think I'm completely insane, I need you to keep quiet until I make it past the front door."*

"You mean, you want me to leave you alone?" Even though the connection was more technical than tangible, he was rather enjoying the closeness—the reflected smiles and light conversation buoyed his spirit in surprising ways, and the unexpected denial of contact hit him like a punch. Would this isolation last minutes, or hours?

She exited the vehicle, then angled a small mirror attached to the side of the car to face her. Her new features did not suit her; the nondescript coiffed blonde hair and mouse brown eyes made her seem ordinary. He'd begun to imagine her only as the version he first met. She produced a slender tube of pale pink lipstick and outlined her thin lips.

"I want you just to listen and watch, that's all. If you see or hear something that I miss, point me in the right direction." After she righted the reflector, she strolled toward the main entryway. *"But I can't talk. Not yet anyway. Just…"*

Her voice trailed off as her hand reached for the door.

"Yes?" he encouraged, hoping she'd complete her thought.

She blew out a steady breath and stared at her warped reflection in the shimmering glass. *"Just wish me luck."*

Zacarias closed his eyes, sending up a silent prayer to any deity listening as she turned the handle and entered the lion's den.

CHAPTER 21

$\mathcal{C}$amille crossed the threshold, shaking the light mist off her hands and heaved a sigh of relief. The lobby was teeming with activity—humans mingled, sipping champagne or coffee, oblivious to the fact they chatted up hideous demons spawned from the very pits of hell. Most of the immortals donned lab coats or lanyards bearing the Zon-Tan logo; not all the employees were otherworldly beings, but enough to seriously tip the balance at the company baseball games. The smell of spoiled milk intermingled with Chanel No. 5 and her stomach threatened to lose its meager contents. Judging by the vapid expressions on the gathered faces, though, no one else must have had her sensitive nose.

A distracted human hostess stood beside a long table filled with name badges of the late-comers. Not wanting to waste another second, Cam hustled over to the reception desk and, after a covert scan of the unclaimed, she formulated her story.

"I am so sorry for being late," she said. "There was a horrible snarl out on River Road and I just managed to squeeze by before they closed it down." She painted on her best smile, patting the rain's wetness from her cheeks. "I'm Annabelle Forrester, representing—"

The frazzled young woman practically threw the name badge at Cam. "That's fine. But I don't know what you want me to do about it." The woman turned away, revealing the ornate Bluetooth earpiece. So much for working on her acting chops. Nodding, Cam pinned the fake name onto her jacket and stepped into the fray. A tuxedoed young man wove between the milling benefactors, offering champagne from a tray. She smiled and, not wishing to be rude, snagged up a delicate flute before he disappeared.

"We're in," she mumbled against the lip of the glass. The flowery sweet bubbles tickled her nose as she took a careful sip.

Surveying the crowd, she was grateful for her choice of attire. Some patrons wore watches costing more than her annual income, but all were dressed in proper business suits.

"There seems to be quite a rogue's gallery in there."

She rolled her eyes at his astute observation. *Thank you, Captain Obvious.*

"Ladies and gentlemen," a voice called out over the din of polite conversation, and she stealthily shushed her distant companion. "If I could have your attention, please. We are ready to begin the tour, so if I could ask you all to gather by the doors. Thank you."

She slugged back the last swallow, then fell into line with the rest of the masses. Time to get a look behind the curtain.

As others filed in behind her, she casually popped onto her tiptoes to canvass the opening doors. She shielded her eyes and swung her head lazily back and forth, appearing as though searching for others in her party, hoping the charade worked while she surveilled all she could for Zacarias.

For the first time, she actually wished he was here to back her up. Rhys would have knocked over the waiters, spilled all the champagne on the electronics, deactivating the whole place. A sad smile touched her lips, but she dismissed the silly sentiment with a slight shake of her head.

The line shuffled onward and she dared a peek behind the reception desk. Just as she'd assumed, the wooden counter hid a bank of various inset monitors. Several screens showed the standard scenes: the front entrance, parts of the lobby, random hallways that appeared and disappeared. Yet what troubled her most was the one monitor crowded with red and gray blobs. She snapped her gaze up to the mirrored surfaces interspersed between the crystal-and-mahogany panels on the walls and confirmed her suspicions. The non-humans appeared as dark shadows on the scan, while the breathing people glowed with life.

No wonder they knew I was human. Curiosity drove her next unvoiced question: What color did the fae reflect?

But she dismissed the notion, turning her attention to the approaching security screening. The double-wide doorframe was supported by a state-of-the-art metal detector, and her stomach knotted as she casually slipped the bag off her shoulder and set it onto the conveyor. With a polite smile, she moved to remove her glasses, only to be halted by the same security guard she'd met last night.

"Those should be fine, ma'am." He offered her a faded version of yesterday's grin.

She wondered what short straw he'd drawn to still be stuck on the job and nodded. Holding her breath, she stepped through the arch. No beeps, pings, or alarms had alerted the masses to her devious devices. Another glance at the machine as she retrieved her bag told her a different story: The friggin' thing wasn't on. Not even a static screen appeared on the blank monitor. The overconfidence in their early warning systems gave her the loophole she needed.

Now safely through their "metal detectors," she entered the laboratory beyond. Ahead lay a long hallway, bisected by busy cross traffic. Doors opened and closed as the entourage meandered down the corridor, and she captured a handful of words from the human tour guide. He was reciting the standard party lines, pointing out the various stock options and returns on investment. Heads nodded and the gathered suits oohed and aahed in the appropriate places. She was more focused on the writings on the individual lab doors, though. None of the symbols were familiar. Fingers crossed, she called in the heavy guns.

"Can you tell what they say?"

Silence. *Did he fall asleep?*

"Zacarias? You still there?" She lagged back, allowing others to slip past her.

"Am I allowed to speak now?"

Even across the connection, his arrogance had rung clear. He wouldn't be half bad if he wasn't such a prick about everything. She readjusted the lens to give him a direct view of the inscription on the door at her back.

"I told you it was just to make sure we made it past their security." She scanned the faces of the interesting blend of humans and monsters and suppressed a shudder. Ignorance could be bliss at times. "So can you read these signs or what?"

"The one at your back is the janitor's closet."

Frowning, she twisted the handle. The door swung inward, away from her, revealing a delightful selection of mops, pails, and brooms.

"Trust me now?"

Smug to a fault, that was certain, and she grumbled, childishly sticking out her tongue even as she nodded and chalked up another point in the Zacarias column. The action was missed by her eavesdropping companion, but it made her feel good. A spare gray jumpsuit hung on a nail and she snatched down the outfit, shoving it inside her bag before shutting the door. Moving one room at a time would take too long; she opted for a quicker method.

"Now, just hang tight, *oui*? Things might get a little blurry for a second." She removed her glasses and held them over her head. "Can you tell which way I should go?"

"Is everything all right here, ma'am?" Three eyes blinked at her from a mottled burgundy face, a cruel mouth twisted into what probably passed for a smile. It had boobs, so it must have been female.

Cam returned the pleasant grin and stretched her arms up, adding an exaggerated yawn. "S'all good. Just needing to finish waking up. Say, could you point me toward the restroom?"

As she put the glasses back on, the monster gestured down an unexplored hall. "It's the first door on your right," she said. "Would you like me to wait for you?"

"*Merci, cher.* Thank you for the offer, but I'll be fine. Just need to toss some water on my face." Cam never understood why that excuse always worked, but she didn't question its power as she headed, un-escorted, toward the obvious bathroom. The only signs she recognized jutting out from the wall were the blue squares adorned with the generic stick man and stick woman. After slipping into the ladies' room, she checked the other stalls and, once certain she was alone, she took the borrowed clothes out of the zippered pouch.

"What exactly do you have in mind?"

She contemplated her options for footwear as she sized up the baggy jumpsuit. "Gonna need to change again," she said. While dancing did not drain her magically, per se, it did take energy and she'd only managed a cup of coffee and some sips of cheap champagne to fuel her body. She was going to end up paying for this double feature later and she prayed the bill would not come due until she was safe at home.

After shimmying out of the form-fitting skirt, she folded up the garment before stowing it in her bag. Just as she'd assumed, the coveralls were huge on her. With a groan, she took off her blazer and it too joined the rest of her hidden ensemble.

It only needs to not fall off me when I walk. That's all. One final item to remove. She groused, then set the glasses onto the sink.

"Don't look," she said.

Dimensions set in her mind, she closed her eyes and willed her body to fit the clothes. Her mother used to shield her from witnessing the actual transformation; she'd be sent out of the room, while other times she'd simply enter a room and discover a new woman there. Fear about what she'd see had kept her younger version from peeking, and she continued the superstition through her entire adult life. Was it hideous? Did her body pull itself apart? She swallowed back the stupid and ill-timed questions and settled in on a bland and forgettable face.

One final push of her magic through her blood, and the dance was complete. She opened her eyes and sighed. It would do for the moment, and that's what mattered. Nondescript. Another face in any crowd.

"That was spectacular." The awe in Zacarias's voice sent shivers along her skin, and not all of them were unpleasant. She glared at the innocent lens on the counter, and her hands flew up to cover her fully clothed lady parts.

"I said not to watch!" Narrowing her eyes at her invisible Peeping Tom, she flipped off the sink then turned toward the door.

"Why did you wish me to look away? Have you never watched yourself dance?" Great. Another convert. Now she'd have to deal with him as well as Rhys with the barrage of questions. She shoved her hands into her pockets and jammed her fingertips into a solid piece of plastic. Her brow furrowed as she grabbed onto the item.

"No way," she muttered, and she stared at the keycard in her open palm. Elated, she draped the looped black cord over her head and giggled gleefully.

"What? What has happened? I cannot see what has you so pleased."

Cam spun with a flourish and jogged over to the sink. "This is our ticket into ... into everything!" She'd over enunciated each syllable, slipping the glasses back on. "It's the employee's keycard. This—" She shook the lanyard for emphasis. "This will probably get us past every locked door."

Most janitors didn't wear heels, but she hadn't brought a second pair of shoes, so she double-checked the length of the pant legs. Once she was certain her feet were completely hidden, Cam headed for the exit.

Cautious, and with fingers crossed, she poked her nose out to peer through the slender gap. The coast appeared clear. With a deep breath, she swung the door open wider and snuck out.

The hallway was eerily unoccupied, and she opted to move quickly down the tiled floor, unsure if the emptiness was a good or bad thing. Her heels tapped out a loud, frustrating tattoo, and she cringed with each step. She switched up her strides instead, tiptoe-running back to the main corridor.

"Why are you sneaking about if your disguise is complete?"

He did have a point. But, unwilling to give him the satisfaction, she came up with a semi-valid excuse. "Because, asshole, I'm kinda scared out of my wits right now." A flash of inspiration sent her looping back on a return path to the original closet, where she grabbed one of the empty wheeled buckets. She set her bag into the bottom, added a mop to complete her guise, and pushed the ensemble into the hall.

"Quite ingenious."

"Fear is a great motivator." Lifting her chin, she aimed her gaze at each passing doorway. "Okay. Your turn. We're looking for anything about disease research, or testing, or..." *Or what? Killer virus that annihilates all kinds of immortals?* Demons in lab coats mingled with human scientists, comparing in murmured voices various notes on clipboards. She picked up the occasional phrase, but her knowledge in the field of biochemistry was limited to the doc talk on "Grey's Anatomy." Not one being she passed in the hall blinked in her direction, much less questioned her destination. Hiding in plain sight. *Works every time.*

"Stop." Zacarias's stern word froze her feet to the floor. *"The corridor on your left. The sign reads 'Viral Development.' Not very discreet, if I do say so myself."*

"Something tells me the tour didn't include this part of the facility." Her gaze swept the scene, and after one deep breath, she tapped her card against the keypad. A soft click and a green light encouraged her heart to beat again. She bit the inside of her cheek to keep her expression neutral. Beyond this door lay another long corridor. At this rate, she'd be lucky to find her way back out of the network of twists and turns.

"There had better be some damned good cheese at the end of this friggin' maze," she mumbled, suppressing the driving instinct to stare at the floor. Answers weren't there; they were emblazoned on the doors she passed at a snail's pace.

Zacarias guided her to lefts and rights, translating the descriptions of the different labs' contents. Various types of research, both above and below industry standards, happened in the pristine, sanitized conditions. Several walls were a mix of solid and see-through, and she peered inside as she strolled along.

Beyond, humans analyzed beakers and test tubes filled with milky liquids. She spied rows of cages, the cries of their inhabitants contained by the thick glass barrier, while demons compared read-outs from charts hanging beside each tortured creature.

"*Mon Dieu*," Cam whispered. "What are they doing to those animals?"

"*That is the virus*," Zacarias answered. "*That's how it starts.*" Cam swallowed hard, sickened by the nightmare only a few feet away. "*The tremors begin small, gradually increasing until the body shakes like a leaf in a thunderstorm.*" He continued to explain the grizzly symptoms as they unfolded before her eyes. Each creature represented a phase in the disease, with the cages along the edge of her periphery motionless and silent.

"So, Z," she interrupted, "if you were the cure, where would you be?"

"Beg your pardon?"

She dragged herself away from the chamber of horrors to continue along her studious path and, checking each window along both sides of the hall, she muttered low, "Think about it. Would you keep the antidote in the same place as the virus, or somewhere else?"

"So you are asking me to imagine myself as an inert substance, or the crazed lunatic who created it?"

She shrugged, not caring if her gesture even registered on Zacarias's radar. "Take your pick. I'm just—"

"ATTENTION. ATTENTION."

Cam's heart jolted into her shoes as the voice boomed out over the internal loudspeakers.

"ONE OF TODAY'S TOUR GUESTS HAS NOT RETURNED TO THE LOBBY." *Busted.* "PLEASE BE ON THE LOOKOUT FOR A MS. ANNABELLE FORRESTER. SHE IS..." Cam heaved a deep sigh while the male voice offered the description of her previous incarnation. Not wishing to tempt fate, she hustled farther down the hall to continue with her search.

"Are you in trouble?"

She dropped her gaze to the ground, avoiding direct eye contact with a particularly hideous apparition. But the creature said nothing as it passed her. Patient, she waited until he was out of earshot before responding.

"No." She sighed. "They're looking for the old me. But I don't know how much time I'll have before we start seriously running out of options."

"I would hide there."

A confused frown tugged her brows together. She stopped her mock mopping. "Huh?"

Imaginary fingers tapped her left shoulder, jerking her gaze over to the thick door beside her. No one stood near, but her heart thundered nonetheless.

"You asked me where I would hide if I were the antivirus." His answer encouraged her lungs to work again. No windows divided the wall; only a keypad was visible. The color scheme of the simplistic symbol was in reverse and was the only markings on the entire barrier. A domed lamp above sat idle. *"In there, I would be safe and unseen."*

"But still close enough to get to if something went wrong. Z, you're a genius." Excited awe filled her voice, and she grabbed her "get into everything" card, buoyed by this new path. She held her breath and tapped the card against the keypad.

Nothing.

She gave the lock another tap. Still nothing. Crap. Not now. She flipped the card over and noticed the black mag strip along the edge. "Please work ... please work ... please work..." Repeating the litany like a prayer, she swiped the card through the slotted side.

A second passed before the overhead light flashed green and the door whooshed open. Immediately, she grabbed the bucket and mop and dashed inside.

The sensation of eyes following her every step crept along her skin. As long as she was dressed for the part, though, she'd be safe. That was the story she'd stick to if she were caught or questioned. The main door dumped her into a small, confining secondary cubicle, where an ominous red light stared at her from the wall. Her hands trembled as she fought off the growing fear of discovery, the debilitating anxiety inching higher the longer she stood in the terrifying silence. An additional second ticked by before blessed air filled the room, and a soft click signaled the return of white lighting. She crossed into the adjoining chamber.

A chilling clunk at her back again ramped up her insides to full-blown panic.

"And just where do you think you're going?"

CHAPTER 22

Camille jerked her gaze around the divided room, frantically searching for the speaker. Cubicles and square research rooms had turned the open space into a labyrinth of possible hiding spots; white chrome walls and thick glass windows reflected both everything and nothing simultaneously. Movement on the far stairway caught her attention. The woman had simply appeared from out of the wall, dressed in a white lab coat, only the click-clack of her heels against the corrugated metal steps breaking the heavy silence. Waves of black curls framed her exotic face, the earmarks of strong Mediterranean roots stamped across each feature.

"Find what you need and get out now. That is Aretina."

She held Cam's gaze as she sauntered down the stairs. "I do not remember calling for any cleaning in here today," Aretina said. With each descending step, Gucci pumps appeared and disappeared beneath the hem of her black, raw silk-and-linen slacks.

Cam readjusted her glasses and dipped her head nervously. "S-sorry, miss. But this isn't my normal shift, and I wasn't sure if—"

A graceful lift of the woman's hand halted any further words. "You are a clever little one, aren't you?" Flashes of golden lightning shimmered in the ebony depths of blacker-than-pitch eyes that regarded her coolly. "But what exactly are you?"

"Pardon?" Cam swallowed hard, blinking rapidly, her fluttering lids keeping pace with her rising pulse.

"*Get out of there, Camille! Get out—now!*" The unaccustomed panic in Zacarias's voice was not helping her to retain her wits.

The other woman began to circle her. "You cannot be fae," she said. "My sensors would have stopped you long before you made it through the front door." Cam remained still, until Aretina leaned in to take a sniff. There, Cam drew the line.

"Okay, that's close enough, *cher*." She stumbled back a step, needing some distance to think. "You normally smell people as a greeting?"

"You are not one of my staff." She winked and tapped her nose. "Your scent is new." The woman dared another inhale, and Cam jerked out of reach. "But there is something vaguely familiar in it. What is your name?"

Cam gaped like a fish, floundering for a viable lie. Nothing came to mind, so she opted for her current cover story. "Annabelle Forrester," she said.

"Annabelle? Ah, the missing guest of this morning's tour. Well, Ms. Forrester. My name is Aretina Mitrou. I am the founder of this research facility." Advance and retreat; one step forward, one step back. The pair waltzed around the sparse furnishings in choreographed synchronicity. Cam shuffled her feet against the slick tiles, smacked her ass into every desk corner within striking distance.

"Research? That's one hell of a name for genocide," Zacarias screamed in her ear, and she was half-tempted to yank out the receiver. Not like he was telling her anything of use. *"The woman is dangerous."* Well, duh? Not many mousy housewives create a toxin deadly enough to annihilate an entire race of people.

"I am very curious, Annabelle," the woman said, "exactly what you expected to find this far off the path."

When a missed cabinet stopped their dangerous tango, Cam halted, still intent on sticking with her current cover story. "I-I guess I just got lost," she stammered, praying her acting chops were good enough. "I mean, this is just a huge maze of—"

"How can not wish them dead...halfling."

Fuck. Cam's thought and Zacarias' voice blended in horrific harmony.

"Seems our kind can breed with humans, after all." Cam held her tongue at the condescending comment about her lineage. "But tell me, do you enjoy being used as a pawn in a game that has nothing to do with you?"

"Nothing to do with me?" She marched right up to Aretina. "YOUR virus killed a dear friend of mine. And ... and another friend is close to joining him. So, I think I have one hell of a stake in the outcome."

A mirthless laugh rang out. "Friend?" The woman splayed a perfectly manicured hand across her bosom, showing off blood red nails and a diamond the size of Kentucky. "I find that very hard to believe. The virus is too powerful for a human to withstand for more than sixteen hours. Only an immortal could still draw breath after being infected. The fae court have no friends, nor do they know the meaning of the word."

Cam unzipped the baggy jumpsuit to her waist, sensing a fight brewing. "Maybe things have changed since you last hung out with them." She shrugged out of the shoulders and tied the long sleeves around her hips.

The room iced over, caught in the woman's frigid stare. "Change," she spat out, as if the taste of the word was too bitter to endure. "Those selfish, conniving beings care naught but for themselves. They have been that way for thousands of years and will continue to be for as long as they draw breath."

Cam faltered, her own mother's warning echoing through the woman's hateful sentiment. During the past couple of days, she'd come to realize she had much to learn about her mother's people. She didn't know everything yet. What she did know was Rhys didn't deserve to die for helping to keep her safe.

"Does that mean all of them should be killed off?" Cam asked. If she could keep the woman talking, maybe she could divert the demoness' pent-up anger long enough for her to reveal the location of the cure. "What about love?"

"Love?" Aretina shrieked, then backhanded Cam, letting her true face slip into the open. Red rimmed the jet orbs, and her pearly whites transformed into crooked rows of shark's teeth. "I gave that bastard my heart." Spittle flew from her thin lips, and her hair swirled around, caught in the tornado of her rage. "I trusted him with all of me, and that whore who dares to call herself queen bats her lashes, and he falls at her feet!"

"Perhaps the womanly heart-to-heart was not the best course of action."

"Gee, ya think?" Cam wiped away the sticky trickle from the

corner of her mouth, rolling her eyes. Any more nuggets of timely advice from Zacarias and she might let the crazy bitch go through with her plan. "How about giving me something more helpful?" she whispered.

"How about, the antidote is in the small cooling unit in the far northern corner. Is that more to your liking?"

She snapped her gaze in Zacarias's whispered directions. "What? Just how in sweet fuck do you know that?" Yet, even as the words slipped from her lips, she caught a glimmer from the area in question—a flare of green, a flash of life hidden in the surrounding death and darkness. Tiny tendrils of light fought against the shadows, instilling her with hope, if only for a moment.

"It is not a hunch, if that is what you are alluding to." His cagey response took her by surprise. If she made it through this, they were going to have a serious talk.

"Oh. You mean the small cooling unit on the other side of the friggin' army of assholes that just showed up?"

"That would be the one."

"Try as you may, my little mystery," Aretina called out over the rapidly approaching boot heels, "you will not be leaving this room alive."

"What, are you scared of a human?" Her foe knew about her mixed ancestry, but not *all* about it. The less she gave away, the better.

With a wave of Aretina's hand, a squad of the reinforcements froze before taking flight. Then bodies scattered like feathers in a wind tunnel, crash landing on desks or anything else in the vicinity. Spines snapped and bodily fluids splashed along the pristine canvas, creating a chilling Jackson Pollack. The remaining guards fled in panic while a new group of hell spawn creatures dressed in crisp uniforms took their place.

"I believe you to be anything but a mere human. However, you have piqued my curiosity." The demon's visage was swallowed up in a blink; features morphed from gruesome to gorgeous faster than Cam could have ever managed the transformation. She had to give the girl props ... or she would, if she wasn't scared out of her mind.

"Sure we can't just talk about this, *cher?*" Cam forced the fear out of her limbs, shook her hands to chase away the tension. No sense in avoiding the fight that was coming, and Cam was heavily outgunned. Didn't mean she was going to just roll over, though.

Aretina strolled closer, a conceited smirk twisting her street-walker red lips. She didn't see Cam as a threat. *Good.* "I don't see how any conversa—"

Cam struck fast, nailing Aretina with a hard right cross, then tucked her arms in tight and added a jaw-snapping uppercut before her opponent could retaliate. She grabbed the nearest object—a keyboard—and slammed it against the back of Aretina's head, and as her foe stumbled, Cam took off at a dead run toward the far cabinet. Eyes on the prize, she scrambled over the carnage and prayed.

A blood-curdling shriek behind her spurred her on even faster. The entire room trembled, then the interior walls exploded, hurtling razor-sharp shards of glass in every direction. Metal fragments joined the lethal darts, slashing at her clothes and her bare arms. Breathing hard, Cam ducked into the nearest cubicle as a desk skated down the narrow path. Winds whipped over her head, hissing hateful words through the open space. She peeked around the corner and immediately regretted the decision.

Her stomach lurched as the mass of mangled bodies twitched. One by one, the deceased jerked about as they took to their feet. Cam swallowed down her rising bile as a nearly headless creature ambled its body around, giving her a glimpse at the head hanging at an impossible angle. No fair. How the hell was she supposed to battle a full-on rage demon with zombie security guards? And with what? Harsh language and a plucky attitude?

"Camille! You must use your magicks!"

"I don't have magic! I AM magic!" she screamed to the voice in her head. Never before had she been upset by her lack of spell ability. If she was in a bind, she simply became someone else—problem solved. Her wits kept her out of any real danger, and she staunchly avoided circumstances involving death or dismemberment.

Yet, with a very pissed-off aerico, a dozen reanimated corpses, and a shit ton of armed monsters between her and the object of this whole excursion, her list of possible disguises was thin.

Another blast rocked her makeshift barrier. One more jolt and she was done for sure.

Zacarias's voice commanded her attention, but survival instinct won out. She spied a rolling chair within arm's reach and kicked the wheeled seat across the floor. The distraction only needed to work for a second. The innocent chair exploded in a ball of flame, and Cam darted in the opposite direction, scurrying on hands and knees closer to the cabinet. A hand clamped around her ankle and yanked her to a halt. She flipped onto her back, kicking and flailing against the undead attacker crawling out from under a pile of debris. Her heel caught on the once human's nose and she drove her leg forward. Destroying the brain worked in every zombie film she'd ever seen; now to test the movie myth. The face folded in, broken bones swallowing her shoe, and the body flopped one last time. She forced down the rising bile and pulled her toes out of its oozing gray matter.

Those were my only good pumps. She tossed the mate away and, fighting the shivers, dove under another desk. Her breathing ratcheted up as she weighed the deadly odds. The antidote was so close; only one row of cubicles separated her from the endgame. Six desks, four short walls, a handful of shambling yet lethal puppets, and about five thousand years of denied wrath in a five-foot-eight package.

"Camille? You have to listen to me."

She slammed her hands over her ears as the explosions grew nearer. Glass bit into her arms, and she cowered deeper under the metal table.

"I can help you. There is a risk, but I believe it will work."

Tears blinded her. The forceful blows from the other side of her flimsy barrier pitched her forward, but she refused to give up her cover. She imagined a pair of strong arms wrapped around her shoulders, banishing her fears, holding her safe.

"Camille? Do you trust me?"

CHAPTER 23

Never before had Zacarias experienced this sensation: Helplessness. He'd heard of it. Witnessed it in the faces of many of his victims. But this was his first encounter on the receiving end of the debilitating response.

And he hated it.

He was glued to the small screen, able to only watch as Camille escaped from danger after danger, and his hands ached, between clenching his fists or slamming his palms loudly onto the table. Apprehension kept him no more than two steps away from the distant views in case he caught something she missed. And her intelligence was astonishing, relying on her quick wits and deductive powers to navigate the labyrinth of corridors. His aid was more in the form of translations, and even that was minor. Yet for all he'd seen during her search, the event he'd carry for the rest of his days was observing her transformation.

She had closed her eyes and had requested he do the same. But the temptation was too great. Nowhere in any of their great histories was a written account of a skin dancer's shift. Rare and beauti-ful, skin dancers were said to have been reclusive creatures who walked easily among the fae and mortal realms, undetected and protected by their malleable anonymity.

He could only gape, transfixed, as each part of her morphed into something different than it was before. Long hair shortened and curled, while olive skin faded into ashen. Her cheeks plumped, and her slight build broadened to fill the baggy jump-suit. A faint golden halo coursed and pulsed around her, the glow fading as her features settled in. When she was safe again in his arms, he'd dig deeper on the subject. First, he would need to get her out of that room.

The image wavered, and he gnashed his teeth. "You say that you have no magic to survive this battle, Camille. If you wish to make it out alive, you must trust me." Debris rained down, blending with the contained smoke and diminishing his visible spectrum even more. The small speaker picked up the moans and groans of the reanimated warriors closing in on her hiding spot.

"I ... *what? How?*" Fear in her voice spurred him into action.

"I can destroy those between you and the cure." He'd asked for her trust, but in truth, he was placing more of him in her hands than he cared to acknowledge; by serving as a conduit for his powers, she'd learn the truth of who, and what, he really was. "Camille, there is no more time. I need your consent to proceed."

This was where he thrived—death magicks. Necromancer, they called him. Such a sinister word for so deep and ancient a power. For centuries, both fae and human bargained with him for vengeance and for retribution. Ending lives was easy for him, yet never did he imagine those skills would help him save anyone, much less a human/fae hybrid and a hapless knight in the service of his queen's conniving sister.

He glanced over to the shivering hulk beneath the sweat-drenched blanket. Would the healer approve of his methods, even if they meant his very survival?

He cared naught for Rhys nor his archaic sense of chivalrous honor. Camille, on the other hand.... Blood pounded through his veins as his thoughts strayed toward his fiery halfling, and he was shocked to discover he was genuinely concerned about how this action would color her opinion of him.

Her panic thrummed along his skin, and his projected embrace did little to comfort either of them. "I will not hurt you," he whispered. A feeble promise. Neither a complete lie, nor the whole truth.

Space. He'd need open space. Without hesitation, he grabbed the computer off the table, as he'd seen Camille do. No cord stopped him as he crossed the room toward the window that opened onto the fire escape. He carefully folded the electronic contraption in half before he climbed the rain-slicked metal stairs outside leading up, in preparation for her acceptance.

"What do I do?" The faraway noises grew louder in his augmented hearing, blasts inching closer to her by the moment.

"I will need to look through your eyes," he said. "Your real eyes," he added in amendment. After jogging up the steps, he carefully placed the slender device beneath a protected overhang, flipped open the screen, and crouched under the sheltering eave. "And I will need to be inside you."

"What!" An especially deafening explosion had echoed in his ears just as he finished his statement, and he chalked up her

shouted question to the booming distraction. *"You need to be where?"*

"We can waste time on long, drawn-out explanations, or do you prefer to live?" Only a distant clap of thunder broke the silence. "Camille?" he said. "I must have your consent."

"I better not regret this in the morning."

"Well, if you say nothing, then you will have no morning. Does that help?" Lightning streaked across the darkened skies, the imminent downpour awaiting his command. He didn't want to frighten her, but he also didn't want her to die in screaming agony.

"Not really," she grumbled and the image dipped up and down.

A smirk touched his lips. "You must say the words, Cam."

Her nickname had slipped off his tongue, and he savored the wild taste of it.

"I consent."

"Thank you." Zacarias removed the mechanical device from around his ear and rose to his feet. With two strides, he stood in storm's furious path, rolled his shoulders, and tapped into his own power.

After his sensual intrusion in her dream last time, he'd maintained the connection, allowing the link to remain open and accessible. His original reasoning was not entirely innocent, and he would have rather kept the second experience as pleasurable as the first. *I will make it up to her.* So, as easily as donning a shirt, Zacarias stepped into Camille's psyche.

Immediately, he was surrounded by her scent. Flowery jasmine blooms intermingled with the cleansing rain and his cock pressed hard against his zipper. Memories flooded in—tangles of scattered thoughts and remembered laughter filled him with a strange peace; tender caresses warmed his skin and breathy moans drove his mind away from the task at hand. He had only a moment to revel in the bliss before her panic had turned the joyride into a chaotic maelstrom. He was battered on all sides, and she nearly shattered the link.

"Camille. Calm yourself. I promised I would not hurt you." He flexed his powers and, taking control of her physical body, he ordered her eyes to open. "Please. You must trust me." Together, they surveyed the scene.

"What are you doing to me?" Tears trailed down her cheek, its sensation mimicking the surrounding cloudburst. He swung his head from side to side, the hazy view giving him detailed locations of all the foes.

He sighed, heart heavy by his necessary actions. "I am saving your life. I will not take anything from you that you are not willing to share." There. That should put her mind at ease. "I am controlling your body, and the more you fight against it, the more difficult this rescue will be."

The tension in her limbs subsided, and as he pushed the connection the final inch, he sensed her recede into herself, her confused spirit slipping out of his reach. With the sync complete, he turned his attention to the surrounding scene. The whipping storm fed his powers. If he'd been given more time, he could have made his way to one of the city's many cemeteries. His mouth watered as he envisioned the untapped wealth of magicks lying dormant in any one of those mausoleums. For now, he'd make do with the angry force of the pelting rain.

Time to poke the bear.

CHAPTER 24

"*A*retina! I see the years have not been kind to you."

Camille recognized the voice coming out of her mouth as not her own. Didn't make it any less weird, though. She'd wondered why Zacarias had been so adamant about her giving her consent. Now she understood. Even giving him direct permission couldn't have prepared her for the tumultuous, yet arousing sensation coursing through her. He was everywhere—walking with her legs, watching through her eyes; his heady scent bombarded her senses, and his strong arms embraced her from within. Stretched too thin, Cam struggled not to think of this newest phenomenon as an invasion.

Her brain could only think of it in sexual terms. After all, he had said he needed to be inside of her, but she hadn't thought he meant sharing the same skin.

What the hell? Zacarias! Panic grew with each passing second, her stomach knotting as she inhaled the sickening and fetid air. After all, it wasn't every day she strolled casually through a room full of zombified guards and an irate demoness. *Much less against my will.*

"*Can you trust me?*" Zacarias's calming tone did little to soothe her jangled nerves.

Not if you're trying to get me killed, Cam countered. His presence filled every inch of her, but would he get her message?

"Zacarias?" The aerico's stunned voice had cut through the crackles and snaps of burning office furniture. "How is this possible? I must double check my security."

Cam dug her heels into the tiles, only to have her marionetted limbs betray her and reveal her hiding spot. Her legs flexed and tensed, his dominating spirit working her body toward danger.

"*Let me handle this, ma minette.*" Zacarias's words swirled in her head as imaginary knuckles brushed against her jaw. She felt like a spectator in her own life as he guided her through the smoldering wreckage. Inside her body, she sat on the verge of hyperventilation as she passed within arm's reach of the idle undead. Their host must have put them on pause while she worked out the mystery. Cam mentally kicked Zacarias under the table, but nothing stopped her forward progress.

"Add as much security as you like, Mitrou," he said. "You know Baltazar made his choice centuries ago. Why can you not accept this and find another to warm your bed?"

How long would she speak with Zacarias's words? She tried to call out from her hiding place, but to no avail. She was trapped; a prisoner in her own skin. Her breathing ratcheted higher, and she felt like throwing up. Through the windows of her own eyes, she could merely stare at the shambling guards and armed demons who slunk closer and, fidgeting helplessly, she prayed for this to end.

The rage demon made another appearance, rows of sharpened teeth bared in a dangerous grin, and dread flooded through Cam even as she stood calmly before the pissed-off aerico. *I've changed my mind, Z!* Apparently, though, after a fae had grabbed the wheel, there were no take-backs.

"Baltazar would have never left me, if your bitch of a queen hadn't poisoned him against me." Spittle had flown from her lips as the self-perpetuating tornado cranked up the A/C in the room. Aretina stalked closer, yet the sounds of shuffling footfalls surrounded Cam on all sides. Zacarias might have been in control, but it was still her body, and any bruises or possible imminent death would be hers to deal with. "I will move on," she continued, "just as soon as she and her treacherous brood are dead. Has the child passed beyond yet?"

Z, move this along and let's get out of here. I really don't want to die here. She recognized a confidence game when she heard one. The demoness was trying to draw Zacarias into her trap, baiting him to drop his guard. And it was working. The temperature crept up, anger radiating from her internal companion.

"Did you have some other place picked out?"

Fucking men.

Cam cursed her lack of actual spell casting ability. If she could have conjured a rabbit out of a hat, she could have created a big enough distraction to sneak out. Instead, she was stuck in enemy territory while Zacarias drove her around like a kid with their first car. The hairs on the back of her neck stood at attention as she sensed the presence of someone, or something, standing too close for comfort. Ice trickled down her spine and a pair of burly arms wrapped around her midsection. Inhuman strength flowed through the limbs crushing her rib cage and the heartbeat pounded a rhythmic and steady tattoo against her shoulder blades.

Instinct snapped to and in her mind, she fought like a lion, kicking her legs wildly, hoping to loosen the tight hold. Her body, however, did not respond. Cam lashed out in her imaginations, screaming, demanding release. Was he going to let her get hugged to death?

"Aretina, this will be my only warning. Stop these attacks or you will not see another day." Zacarias's voice had betrayed none of the oxygen deprivation she was feeling. He could have at least sound winded. Pinpricks of light swam in her vision as the aerico moved out of her field of vision.

Before darkness swallowed her whole, Cam prayed one single word, hoping Zacarias was listening: *Please.*

"You will do what?" Aretina appeared directly in front of her face, haughty, assured of her victory.

"This."

With one word from Zacarias, the pressure on her lungs vanished. The arms around her blackened, withered before her eyes, but it was *her* hand that gripped the sneaky assailant's forearm, the fiery streams emanating from her own pale fingers. As she spun about to face her attacker, she could no longer tell if it was male or female as howls of unspeakable agony poured out of its twisted and tortured mouth. Facial features dissolved, melted by the unstoppable heat of Zacarias's powerful magic.

Howling enraged, the demoness waved more guards to join the fray while she hid behind the ever-growing living shield.

Rhys had warned her, but she'd refused to believe him. Now, she was forced to watch as Zacarias unleashed the true necromancer within, calling the life out of his reanimated victims with nothing more than a touch of her hand. She sensed the cries of their harvested souls burning her heart like acid.

Zacarias swept through the waves of guards, determined and relentless, taking neither pity nor mercy on anyone, with her arms extended and fingers splayed out before her. Bodies convulsed and twitched. Limbs bent inward and collapsed, forms contorting and shrinking into piles of blood-soaked clothes. Even the reanimated corpses did his bidding, attacking the uniformed men and women racing for an exit.

Stop, stop. Oh, God. Please stop.

Shots rang out. Bullets whizzed past her. A barrel aimed directly at her face wavered before the arm holding it steady snapped in two. Power pulsed out of her, solidified, becoming her own personal magical Kevlar shield. Screams and gurgling death throes echoed through the room, reverberating off the gore-splattered glass, and Cam was helpless to protect herself from the carnage. Her hands wouldn't respond to cover her ears, nor would her eyelids snap shut. Quivering and sobbing in the corner of her mind, she cursed Zacarias in every language she knew and made up some new ones just on principle alone.

"Give my regards to Tannequil when you meet her on the other side," Aretina screamed above the din of the dying. "The queen is dead," Aretina exclaimed. "Long live the queen!"

Time ceased to have a purpose other than to provide more fodder for Zacarias's lust for devastation, and Cam cried out, praying for the guards to stop coming. The whole place reeked of burnt flesh and melted plastic, and her brain warned her she would throw up as soon as her body was again under her control. She'd lost track of the aerico, but she did not see her white lab coat among the dismembered, the disemboweled, or the disintegrated.

Zacarias, please. Stop. Her soft plea had finally hit the mark. Her gaze swung around the decimated laboratory. Charred limbs jutted out, reaching toward salvation yet receiving none. *I did this. I let this happen.* The swirling, pulsating energies shifted flow, turning inward to surround her.

"Are you hurt?" Tenderness and concern laced his words, but she was way past consolation. Retreating as far as she could within her mind, Cam refused to give him access to her heart, and she struggled to wipe away the visions seared into her memories.

"Camille? Were you injured?" Ethereal fingertips brushed against her arms while a warm presence stood at her back. Anger and grief had mixed to create a dangerous cocktail of emotions. Her muscles tensed, and she was eager to lash out at something—anything. The drive to fight churned inside her, and his unexpected gentleness had only fueled the fires.

Why? Tears stung her eyes, burned like embers down her cheeks. All those lives. All those people, gone. In defense of his slaughter, the rational part of her mind used the argument of their being employed by an evil entity and trying to kill her. But families would wait tonight for loved ones who'd never come home. These people had been someone's mother or father, wife or husband.

In all her long years, she'd managed to stay out of every major conflict. During the American Civil War, she'd been traveling along the Mediterranean coast, in the company of a lovely group of gypsies. When, at the beginning of the twentieth century, things had begun to get dicey in Europe, she'd followed the old Silk Road and had found peace in the Far East. She'd lived by her wits and her ability to blend in. Now, in this moment, she felt exposed. Raw and open, like a wound. Her body may still have been safe, but inside, she was broken.

Through her, Zacarias had wrought destruction of biblical proportions.

"It was the only way to—"

No. She was in no mood, even as she knew his sensible explanation to be the truth. His embrace still held firm, unwilling to let her escape from his presence no matter how much she protested. *It was not the only way. It was the way you wanted. All I needed was a path to get the cure and get out. I never asked for ... for this.*

Cam nudged her chin toward the smoking ruins. *Had any of it been necessary?*

"I was only trying to protect you."

The stairs leading to the refrigerated unit housing the reason for this whole trip were feet away. She merely had to skirt around the broken bodies and shattered desks. She swallowed hard against the resurfacing urge to vomit. Humans and monsters lay in the scattered wreckage, and her "give a shit" meter had finally reached its limit.

Get out.

His comforting energies were now wasted on her, his benevolent actions useless in the face of her inner turmoil. Her hands clenched into fists, arms vibrating with pent-up frustration. *I said GET OUT!* And she screamed out in anguished fury.

The second heartbeat in her chest vanished, and she fell to her knees. Glass cut into her palms, the pain centering her. No longer filtered through Zacarias, the full brunt of the true devastation hit her square in the face, and she emptied the meager contents of her stomach in record time, continuing to dry heave with each noxious breath she drew. Salty tears coated her lips and gave her little solace. With stuttered inhales, she wiped off her mouth with the back of one trembling hand.

"Camille, I…"

Brushing away the buzz in her ear, she weakly climbed to her feet. She tried using her eyelids as makeshift wipers, but the raining tears simply wouldn't let up. She should be grateful to him. She was still very much alive and was about to get what she needed to rid her of all the meddling fae in her life. But she wasn't sure if she could balance the cost within her soul.

Cam searched through the rubble for any sign of a white lab coat, but she found nothing. "Sh-she's not here." An invisible hand caressed her cheek, and she pushed at the empty air. "Please. Don't." If this was his way of apologizing, he would be in for a huge surprise when they were once again face to face.

She woodenly lumbered over to the semi-intact glass-encased unit, where a keypad beside the door troubled her for only a second. Her first thought was to scan the card still hanging around her neck, but apparently having a gazillion volts of death magic blasted through it had wiped the mag strip. *Who'da thunk it?* She scanned the nearby clutter, hoping to find another viable key.

A shadow caught her eye, and she swung her gaze toward the shifting movement. It took a couple of blinks before she realized it was her own reflection. She wanted to blame the warped chrome for her surreal appearance, but that would be a lie. Soot smudges and the handful of small scratches on her cheeks had been cut clean by the slender silver rivulets dripping off her chin. Some-where along the way, she'd lost her opening disguise, and her own green eyes stared back at her. At least, she believed they were hers. The color was almost right, yet they were empty, haunted by the violence she'd witnessed. Her hair was a complete rat's nest; it would take a weed whacker to hack through all the knots and snarls. Magic only did so much for her; the rest, she left in the hands of Paul Mitchell. She added it to the list of things she would do the minute she got back to her place, filing it right after *Heal Rhys* and before *Kick Zacarias's ass*.

A melted metal table leg doubled as a club, and she smashed the barrier with ease. Gaining the prize was a hollow victory. Drained of all emotions, she reached through the shattered glass and pried open the door. Red dripped off her fingertips and smeared along the handle. Normally, the sting along her forearm would cause her alarm, but she only stared, numb, at the blood oozing from a handful of claw-like gouges. *Worry about it later*, she told herself. *Just get what you need and get the hell out. Eyes on the target.*

Cam lifted her gaze. In the entire unit, only one box of delicate vials was housed, each tube bearing the same symbol. Sighing, she retrieved the samples. No choirs of angels sang out, nor did any rousing applause fill the room. In fact, the silence was unnerving. *So much for the big finish.* She'd expected sirens and klaxons, shouts from security, but instead there was ... nothing. Were the lab areas soundproof? The only place she'd heard voices were the hallways; each room beyond the glass walls was a complete secret.

She reveled in the unbroken peace for another minute before the need to escape tapped her on the shoulder. Did she have an out? She spied the mop and the bucket by the entrance; the pair had been spared from annihilation somehow. Her disguise, however, hadn't fared so well. Scorch marks and blood spatters created a ghoulish polka dot pattern against the flattering charcoal jumpsuit.

"Perhaps there is a..."

Again, she waved off his assistance.

"I don't need any more help from you," she said, choking on

the words as she shuffled her bare feet over to the standard red fire alarm lever on the far wall. One quick yank, and she got her sirens. Lights flashed, blinking from red to white, and the door clicked open. Cam recovered her bag, calm and measured, and stowed the serum safely inside the large pocket. The open doorway poured her into the bustling employees seeking the nearest exit and, melting into the panicked throng, she slipped out to cut across the parking lot toward her vehicle.

"I've got it, and I'm coming back," she mumbled, gunning the engine and pulling out of the narrow spot. Before Zacarias could add anything, she yanked the receiver out of her ear and threw it out the window.

CHAPTER 25

Miles blurred by as Camille returned on automatic pilot. She obeyed every posted speed limit and had even slowed for the yellow lights along Rampart. Honks and obscene gestures aimed at her little sedan punctuated her journey until she'd pulled into her normal parking space, where she cut the engine and sat in the enveloping silence. The pungent stench of burning office furniture and overcooked meat refused to leave. She'd slipped out of the wasted overalls and had driven on, wearing only her ruined tank and a pair of shorts she kept stowed in the back seat. Her feet ached, their soles slashed raw after her escape, and the thought of trudging along the rain-slicked pavement wasn't filling her heart with glee.

At the moment, nothing filled her heart with glee, or with anything for that matter. Her soul had been sucked dry, and she shuffled through the motions of living. No matter how tightly she squeezed shut her eyes, images of the writhing guards dying a slow and torturous death refused to dim. The company might have been involved in malignant clandestine ventures, but was every employee guilty? Was the blanket of blind punishment justified?

"Dammit," she muttered and dashed away a new fall of tears. Her crisis of faith would have to take a back seat. Her friend was on borrowed time, and to save his life, she'd have to get her ass out of her car. Swallowing hard, Cam found her spine and opened the door. The humid evening air kissed her cheek, promising another wet night, and she welcomed it. Maybe the rain would wash away the darkness she couldn't seem to shake.

He saved your friggin' life. Why are you freaking out about it? She climbed out after snatching her bag off the passenger seat and limped to her trunk. Zacarias had promised to keep her safe, and he'd been true to his word. All her injuries had occurred after she'd demanded he give control back to her. Why was she so angry?

Digging through the random items, she fished out a pair of beat-up cross trainers, then clenched her jaw as she shoved her feet into the ragged sneaks. Her ensemble was horrific at best, but she didn't care. Her destination was a few blocks away and it was time to get rid of her cargo.

A sinking feeling churned in her gut. She'd cut off Zacarias after leaving the parking lot and had used the drive back to sort through her chaotic pile of emotions. But in her anger, she'd forgotten she no longer had any connection to know of Rhys's condition. Was he still alive? Had he died while she wallowed in her childish pout?

Cam slammed the trunk, fumbled with the keys to secure her vehicle. A series of short, sharp tweets encouraged her to turn toward home, and she forced her brain to ignore each painful step, concentrating instead on getting the necessary antidote up to her friend.

Rhys had done everything to protect her; now, she needed to make good on her end. In an ungraceful blend of limping and jogging, she hobbled to the back alley and up the stairs, holding each whimper behind clenched teeth with each shift of weight. The two short flights seemed to climb upward for days and she pulled herself up the railings for the final steps. The rain didn't start until she reached her open window, and by the time she'd crawled through it, she was soaked.

"I've, aah—" She hissed, pain stealing her remaining strength, and her knees buckled the instant her feet hit the solid floor. To her surprise, though, she didn't land in a heap. Instead, a strong pair of arms had scooped her up and carried her to the nearest chair.

Zacarias deftly unlaced the sloppy knots and carefully removed her blood-soaked shoes. She reached out, stilled his fingers, and he lifted his head, a confused mix of emotions flashing in his electric blue depths. Exhaustion had painted shadows along his high cheekbones and dark circles had ringed his forlorn eyes. She wasn't sure, but there might have been a hint of an apology floating around in there. She'd think on it later. *Priorities.*

"Don't worry about me." She slipped the bag off her shoulder and pushed back to her feet, wincing with each shuffled step. "I need to take care of Rhys first. Besides, we need to see if this is the right thing after all."

Zacarias held her gaze, frozen in his crouch. *This is the same man who just vaporized about two dozen people, using you as the weapon.* Yet, as he knelt at her feet, she saw the savage necromancer, the Grand Enforcer, and her passionate fantasy lover all inhabiting the same body. And she didn't know which version of him to trust at the moment. She looked away, set her sights on the wheezing, shuddering body beneath the blanket.

Thankfully, she was near enough, and only two staggers were required to pull herself to the couch, where she collapsed once again, her ass hitting the coffee table as an impromptu seat. After rummaging through her bag, she carefully removed the object of the whole trip. The small box of ampoules was intact, and upon closer inspection, she even found a syringe included. Everything she needed, except one tiny thing: an amount.

She stared at the scribbles on the white label, willing the knowledge to seep into her brain.

"Is the number you are seeking 7cc? Does that make sense?"

Cam ping-ponged her gaze between the silent glass tube and Zacarias as he leaned over her shoulder. How the hell...? "You can read Latin."

"I can read Latin." He'd echoed her backward realization with about the same degree of enthusiasm as her initiating statement. He moved away from her and claimed her vacated seat, his long legs easily crossing the gap to rest beside her on the low table. Cam frowned, confused not by his lazy repose, but by his damp hair.

"How did you...? Never mind." She returned her waning focus to saving her friend. Grateful for all those nights spent watching medical procedurals, Cam slid the needle into the rubber stopper. The bottle wobbled and, swearing, she tightened her grip to steady the process. Zacarias shifted into her periphery and she jerked her hand up, halting any assumed assistance.

I can do this... I can do this... She carefully drew out the pale amber liquid.

Now what? Did she stick him in the arm? In the ass? Would it even make a difference? His weak moan and a rattling breath forced her into a quick decision and, exposing the meat of his bicep, she stuck the long needle in and depressed the plunger. She called on her Hollywood knowledge of medicine and massaged the spot, hoping it actually did help to spread the potentially healing tonic. Either that, or she'd just sealed his doom.

She silently studied her unconscious friend, while the snakes in her gut writhed in faster and tighter circles. Her jaw locked, and her patience began to grow thin as she waited for a sign that the elixir had hit its mark.

"How long?"

Cam had almost forgotten about Zacarias. His odd half question confused her. Actually, she was trying very hard to push him as far as possible from her thoughts.

"How long what?" She refused to look away from Rhys. He was still so jaundiced, as though the couch and the blanket were stealing his coloring. Took a couple moments for her to dissect Zacarias's query; even shorter for her impatient brain to spit out an answer. "How the hell am I supposed to know that? Not as if they have any directions on this."

"Camille, I—"

"Oh, wait." The turbulent emotional roller coaster forced her out of her guarded crouch and she shot to her feet. "It does have directions; they're just in Latin, which you happen to read." Her body screamed with each movement, muscles tender and aching. "So how about *you* tell *me* how long I'll have to wait to find out if I killed him or saved his friggin' life?"

Why was everything so loud? No, it was just her. Zacarias took to his feet and regarded her from beneath hooded eyelids, his white-and-golden blond hair framing his ethereal features. She blinked away the angered tears while her mind processed the scene. He stood before her as a true fae—no glamour masked his inhuman beauty—and her heart thundered in response. His clothes were soaked, but it hadn't rained as far as she knew until she'd gotten back.

He dared a couple of steps closer and gently wrapped his fingers around her shoulders. "If there is something I have done to upset you..."

Astonished, she gaped. "Something? You slaughtered all those people in there!" Feebly, she sought to loosen herself from his embrace. Except for the small points of contact between them, everything hurt. She needed her anger, and she used it like a weapon. Standing this close to the full glory of the Grand Enforcer of the Fae Queen, she needed some kind of defense. Her palms pressed flat against his damp shirt, the warmth of his skin and the beat of his strong heart tempting her into an unwanted tranquility. She should push him away, should throw him out the damned window and be done with him.

A confused furrow cut across his perfect brow. "Slaughtered?" he said. "Is that how you perceived my help?"

"Help? You asked me to trust you and ... and..." Her chin quivered, while her inner voices argued vehemently.

"Would you have preferred I let them kill you instead? Would that solution have met your approval?" She sensed his anger simmering just beneath the surface, yet his words lacked any dangerous force. He was right. She wasn't acting very appreciative of his saving her ass.

"No, but ... I mean, thank you. I just..." Emotions entangled her words and the resultant stalled speech only added to her frustrations. "Dammit, Z. Do you know how it feels to be so helpless?"

"Helpless?" he said, and an eerie fire lit the cerulean blue pools above her. A shudder ran down her spine. "You force me to watch, through your eyes and still miles away from your actual location. All the while, you take chances with your life, and with the lives of my people, and you tell me I do not understand helplessness?"

"You couldn't go in there and you knew it," she retorted, arguing to keep herself from falling into his arms. God, he was gorgeous. She shouldn't have noticed it at a time like this, but his raw sensuality was nearly too much for her to dismiss. "I didn't take undo risks," she said. "I—"

"You got lucky," he said, and his bitter words cut her to the bone. Again, he was right. Sheer dumb luck had allowed her to stumble into the janitor's closet and find the keycard. She'd made it to the final lab through a series of fortunate events, but the fates themselves had only let her make it that far. After that, she'd needed to call in for backup. "Time and time again," he went on, "you were blessed until you painted yourself into a corner with no way out. That is what I would consider an undue risk."

Cam bit down on the inside of her cheek, holding in her snark, especially after hearing her own words parroted back. "I was following your directions, Einstein. Remember, I can't read Greek." *So I didn't succeed too well*, she mused, and she turned her gaze away, twisting her shoulders in the same direction. Too bad a solid pair of unyielding arms gave her no quarter.

"Cam, why are you so angry with me?"

Why did he have to sound like he really gave a shit? His unexpected tenderness teetered her resolve, opened a crack in the emotional floodgates.

"Because I have to be angry at something," she blurted out. Stupid logic, but that didn't make the sentiment any less true. "I've been shot at, attacked by zombies, stood toe to toe with the picture of a psycho woman scorned. Then, I become a prisoner in my own skin while I act as a lightning rod for phenomenal cosmic powers." Images before her blurred as tears veiled her vision. "I feel empty, exhausted, and confused. I'm hungry. I'm soaked. You're soaked," she added, tossing her hand his direction. "My feet hurt." *Great. Now I'm whining.* "And I don't even know if the crap I brought back is gonna work."

Her elbows buckled, and she face planted into Zacarias' chest, sobbing at last.

CHAPTER 26

Finally.

Zacarias heaved a sigh of relief and wrapped his arms around Camille's trembling shoulders. The moment she'd entered the apartment, he'd sensed her all-consuming rage, unfocused and erratic. Her moods had swung from reticent to angered and back with each step she'd taken. He found himself once again in the position of outside observer. She'd paced around the apartment like a caged beast, wild and panicked, and he could only ask probing questions, hoping he landed on target soon.

When he'd entered through their link, he'd sensed her resistance. She had allowed him just enough access to channel his powers but had remained out of reach and unconnected. In his world, faes blended their magicks practically on a daily basis, sharing power for the mundane and for the exotic. Sexual encounters experienced in the midst of a deep link were addictive, to say the least; the total surrender and absolute erotic pleasures both given and received became a high more dangerous than any drug known by mortals and immortals alike. Humans fell under the seductive spell much easier, their minds so simple to manipulate. The skill came in handy to keep up the myths surrounding his brethren and their darker appetites.

Perhaps she'd never linked with another before, which might explain her distance during the experience. Yet even as he reviewed the exact prior happenings, he couldn't discover anything that would have caused her such distress. He'd honored his word—he hadn't hurt her, nor had he allowed her to be hurt. He'd even stayed out of the private part where she'd hidden. The refuge in her psyche had been visible to him; nothing more than a cozy glass closet that gave her both protection and an open view of all that transpired. He'd done nothing wrong, as far as he knew.

Her refusal of his assistance, however, combined with her demand to break their link told a much different story. Once freed, she'd walled herself off, even going so far as to remove the technological devices that had allowed them to speak directly.

Apparently, she did not approve of his methods of dealing with the enemy. He'd been working on his apology before she had returned. Now, as she came undone in his arms, it was quite clear that more than a simple "I'm sorry" was needed. Her heavy sobs split the silence, and he stroked his fingers lightly along her spine. She quaked in his embrace, clinging to his damp shirt.

"Shh... You carry too much on your shoulders, *ma minette*. None of the burden is yours to bear."

She'd confessed her helplessness, and he was shocked by his own truthful admission of a similar sensation. To be honest, it scared him in some deep part of his soul more than he dared to admit. If others in the court were to discover his affections, Camille would be used as a bargaining chip against him. He was already certain she was none too happy about being a pawn in this simple chess match; imagine how she'd react learning his feelings toward her had tied her to a fate worse than the horrors she had just witnessed.

Zacarias buried his fledgling love even as he sought to soothe her ragged nerves. Her soft curves melted against his body, diverting his mind from the task at hand, and as he threaded his fingers through her tousled hair, the rich fragrance of honeysuckle and spring rain wreathed his senses. His mouth watered. Smoke and death still lingered in her tresses, though, and a twinge of guilt tapped on his conscience. He rested his cheek on the crown of her head.

Her sobs had subsided, but he wasn't ready to release her quite yet. The peaceful moment calmed his divided heart. She claimed to have no powers, but he disagreed. *I am magic,* she'd said. Bold and true words. She held sorcery unlike any he'd ever come across in his long years—pure and invigorating. Her untapped potential could be limitless, perhaps even a rival for the ruling family. He tightened his embrace, using her presence to banish his dangerous thought.

Apologies had never been his forte. He was a man of action, though somehow he didn't think a roll in the sack would be the right solution. With a tender touch on her chin, he guided her eyes up and fell into her pools of turbulent green.

"Camille, I..." He paused. How best to proceed? He searched her face, reading every subtle clue, interpreting each breath. A delicate blush painted the apples of her cheeks, and he lowered his head, intent to sample her lips...

... when a strangled gasp from the couch sucked all the air out of the room and shattered the mood. Her eyes flared wide, and she snapped her gaze away, her thick hair whipping him in the face as she scrambled out of his embrace. Bereft, he dropped his empty arms and leveled a perturbed glare at the interruption.

"Oh, good. You're awake."

Darkness and pain receded gradually until Rhys could breathe without an agonizing fire burning in his lungs. With each deep inhale, the anvil weighing on his chest vanished until his heart beat easily. Had he died? Was this what the fates had in store for him beyond the Veil?

The dripping, venomous sarcasm from the Grand Enforcer's words, however, alerted him of his actual location. No way would that bastard allow himself to die, and Rhys was quite certain Zacarias wouldn't bother with the likes of him upon his demise. He was alive, and improving as the seconds ticked on.

"Wh ... what has happened?" He coughed to clear the lingering death from his throat. He'd barely peeled back his eyelids, when a more welcome and comforting weight had stolen his breath. This shift, he accepted happily.

"You're alive! You're okay!" Camille squeezed him, and he was grateful to be able to return the gesture. He sank into the simple embrace, relishing the joy in her voice. Perhaps things were truly looking up.

Until the rapid fall of painful blows to the meat of his arm told him otherwise. He drew his eyebrows together and fixed his gaze at the beauty lying across him.

"You scared the ever-living shit out of me." Her beautiful green eyes were ringed with black soot and rimmed in puffy red, and trails of very recent tears still glistened fresh on her bruised and nicked cheeks. Her appearance was noticeably haggard, and her hair reeked of smoke and dark magic. "You drop like a stone in the damned kitchen, and then you get this-this... This!"

She yanked his hand out from underneath the blanket, exposing the fading trails of blackened veins. The sight turned his stomach. He had no idea the venom had progressed to such a state. He reached out, hoping to comfort her with a tender caress, but she scuttled out of his limited range.

"You, you lie on my couch, groaning and moaning, dying, as far as I know."

Rhys scooted up to a more seated position. His body ached but was eager for the movement. Camille's frantic energy frightened him more than the past potential of his own early demise. A shadow clung to her, even in the bright fluorescent light of the open living room, and the fact that the shade matched quite closely to the Grand Enforcer's aura squeezed the tightening knot in his gut.

Concerned, he caught her uneven steps as she limped toward the kitchen. "Camille," he said, "you are hurt?"

She answered with a lazy, backhanded wave, but he read more in the pale knuckles that gripped the counter. Rhys struggled to climb off the sofa, determined to fulfill his knightly duties.

"I thought you would keep her safe." He refused to censor his accusatory tone toward the necromancer as he glanced sidelong at the man. Something had transpired between Zacarias and Camille, leaving both guarded and on edge.

Zacarias folded his arms across his chest. "She breathes. Is that not safe enough?"

Why didn't...? Oh. Camille was still injured because the

Grand Enforcer's magicks did not allow him to cure. For once, he actually pitied his adversary. Centuries of doing the queen's dirty work had tapped the light from Zacarias's powers, leaving only darkness as his reservoir.

"Why did you not rouse me upon her return?" he said, and he cringed as soon as the words had tripped off his tongue. The perfectly matched pair of perplexed eyes pinned him to the floor and only echoed his own mental chastising.

Camille barked out a hollow laugh. "And here I thought that was what we did. What was I thinking?" She took another wobbly step before grabbing onto the short countertop and pulling herself into a nearby chair. Rhys searched for the source of her pain, the answer to which came in the form of a grotesque pattern of small bloody footprints, starting on the pale blond wood beside the window, reappearing beside the couch, and terminating at the pristine tiles beneath her current perch. The sight chilled his blood, and he dashed over to her.

"Camille?" Her defiant body language told him to proceed with caution, and only with her permission. "I can help you. Will you allow me to heal you?" The baggy, tattered pant legs had swallowed her own legs, but the rust-stained hems spoke volumes.

She blatantly ignored him as she examined the bottom of her lacerated foot, where shards of glass still protruded in various spots. She pinched one, tugged at it as she hissed in pain.

He stilled her trembling fingers. "Camille. You have saved me." His honest statement drew her gaze away from her grizzly task. "Please," he said, "allow me to return the favor in some small measure."

"If I can get the glass out, it'll heal on its own," she explained woodenly. No emotions laced her once bright green eyes, and his heart ached to see her so lost.

A shadow fell over them as Zacarias moved to stand at her side, and he placed his hand on her shoulder. "You will be in agony until then. Let the knight do his work."

There was no command or push in Zacarias's voice, and Rhys lifted his gaze, surprised to see the Grand Enforcer, normally proud and aloof, now compassionate and accommodating. Never before had Zacarias given his skills any credence. Had his nearly dying earned the man's respect? Upon closer inspection, however, he realized the show of emotions was directed to one and only one person.

Rhys tucked the new and potentially dangerous piece of information away and, with a slight dip of his chin, he returned his attentions to Camille. Her head drooped, hanging heavy off her neck. He squeezed her fingers lightly, waited for her response. His mind harkened back to the events in the hospital. He hadn't asked for permission from the children; however, he had yet to encounter one person in an infirm ward who did not wish to be healed. She would have the final say in this, and he must honor her wishes no matter how much his heart would ache should she refuse.

Time crept by and Rhys thought perhaps she'd fallen asleep, until an exhausted sigh slipped from her lips, and she nodded. Before she changed her mind, he closed his eyes and sent a wave of healing magicks through their simple contact. He followed the pulse, guiding it toward the ragged soles of her feet to push out the fragments of glass, metal, and other sharp objects, the shards tinkling against the porcelain tiles like a sudden rain burst. Then he searched further, discovering the faint traces of a brawl. The injuries were only moments older than the cuts on her feet and just as easy to remedy. But the darkness that lingered along her spirit was neither damage nor wound, and she clung to it as though she wanted to hold on to the sensation, as if reveling in the pain it caused.

He wanted to heal her completely, to give her the same gift she'd bestowed upon him. She deserved to have her joy returned. But he could only mend matters of the physical. Matters of the heart were beyond his powers.

When he was certain she would no longer feel pain from her injuries, Rhys called back his magicks and knelt beside her.

"You've done your good deeds for the day," she said, speaking to the floor, her voice hushed and detached. "Now, please, leave me alone."

"Camille, I—"

She fled from her chair, cautiously sidestepping the scattered debris, and stood in the center of the living room.

"Look," she continued, "you got what you came here for, and you know it works." She grabbed an odd box from the table beside the couch and crossed back to them, despair and anger reflected in her eyes. She shoved the package into Zacarias's hands. "Just take it and go."

Rhys levered himself sluggishly off the floor, his body still drained from the ravaging illness, his powers slow in returning. With the aid of nearby furniture, he finally regained his feet and stood beside Zacarias, the pair of them sharing the confused moment.

"But how can it—"

Camille jerked her frigid stare to Rhys. "You can figure that out without me. My part of the bargain has been fulfilled. Now, go. I just want to be left alone."

Desperation had tainted her words, and Rhys was afraid she'd break down if they left. He was more concerned, though, by what she'd do if they stayed. He turned his gaze toward the silent Grand Enforcer at his side. No glamour masked his appearance, and still the man hid behind invisible walls. Whatever had transpired between the two of them while they'd quested for the cure would remain a secret only they shared. Rhys sensed it was far from over, though.

He dared one final glance at Camille. Strong and capable, the skin dancer held her ground, with only a hint of unshed tears shimmering in her creamy emerald eyes. He softened his expression and touched her hand gently. Her jaw tensed, and she did not move to return the gesture. Instead, Rhys offered a weak smile, then nodded as he dropped his arm to his side.

Zacarias gripped his shoulder and, without another word, Camille and her small apartment vanished.

CHAPTER 27

"Oy! Earth to Cam! Order up, *chère!*"

Camille blinked back to the present and sniffed away the latest bout of sadness. Three days had passed since Zacarias and Rhys had beamed out of her place, leaving her adrift in a sea of turbulent emotions. She'd demanded they go, and the moment they'd winked out of existence, she'd dropped to her knees and sobbed. She'd blamed the cathartic breakdown on the shit-tastic day she'd just survived; fighting off demons and hordes of the undead were not her usual Friday plans. Pile onto that the resurrection of her friend and the surprising yet terrifying tenderness from the powerful Grand Enforcer, and she'd been shocked her resolve to remain standing had lasted as long as it had.

She didn't know how long she'd stayed curled up in a ball on the floor, wailing like a baby. Exhaustion had taken over at some point and she'd woken up with the midday sun streaming through her half-open window. Mechanically, she'd climbed up off the rust-brown-spotted wooden floor—*The movies never quite get dried blood right*—and the random thought had helped to kick her body into gear. She'd pondered further on the innocuous matter as she gathered the cleaning supplies from under the kitchen sink.

The mundane task of scrubbing away the evidence of the previous day's events had done nothing to banish the deep emptiness. Zacarias had been truthful with her, scarily so, during every step of their symbiotic journey. He'd fulfilled his promise and had brought her out of that room alive. Her own senseless and baseless fears had mucked everything up. Her parents had instilled in her such a deep apprehension when dealing with any immortals; so entrenched was this, in fact, she refused to see beyond her preconceived ideas of her extended ethereal family. Rhys and Zacarias never had a chance to prove or disprove her prejudices.

She'd opted to remain among humans because they were safe. They eventually aged and died, taking with them any knowledge or secrets they had gained through their limited years. She'd made and remade herself in their world so many times, she actually had to keep a written log of names, identities, and places she'd lived so she could keep her story straight should she ever return. In their world, she was nothing out of the ordinary, and she enjoyed the anonymity.

If she'd lived in the fae realm of her mother's people, she would have forever been branded as a freak, never wholly belonging with them, and she would have been ostracized and viewed as a mistake. For this reason, among many others, she'd sent away the two men. They belonged in that other world, and the sooner she'd slammed the door on her dreams of a happily ever after with one particular fae, the sooner she could get back to her life.

And for the past three days, she had almost convinced herself she could do it. She'd returned to work that same night. A small memorial sat on the corner of the bar for Deacon, complete with a vodka tonic and his signature spectators. Photos of him from various times in his life adorned the scene, peeking out above the candles and the wilting flowers.

Big Rob had welcomed her with a warm hug as he told her of Deacon's passing. She responded accordingly, returning the unaccustomed tenderness from her boss, and she'd shed a couple of tears. The ploy was more for her benefit than his. If her fellow employees believed she was mourning the passing of their kindly patron, maybe she could get away with the occasional breakdown.

Her plan had worked for a short time. When she found herself sobbing while refilling the ice, though, she had to face facts. Zacarias and Rhys had both managed to worm their way into her life and into her heart, and she was miserable without the both of them.

Rhys, her stalwart knight, compassionate and curious, had become her trusted confidant, and his fresh innocence never failed to make her smile.

Zacarias....

Zacarias was an entirely different matter. He was danger. From the moment he'd swaggered up to the bar, he'd called to her blood with a frightening intensity. Her head screamed for her to keep her distance, to kick him to the curb, and to set her sights on safe Rhys. Too bad her heart had refused to listen. She wasn't going to give in too easily, but his dark and sensual magic had truly ensnared her, and she hated to admit how much she missed him.

"Where you at, *miouche?*" Big Rob peered at her through the pass-thru window, his bushy brows creating a heavy ledge over his concerned blue eyes.

Cam dashed the back of her hand across her leaking eyes and reached for the steaming dish. "I'm here, I'm here," she said, and she painted on a half-hearted smile. But he wasn't buying it. Heaving a great sigh, she dropped her arm and rested the edge of her hand on the open frame. "*Desole, cher.* Sorry I ain't been myself quite lately."

"Family troubles?"

Family. She'd fabricated the story of her cousin to protect Rhys. Now, the cover was becoming truer than she wanted to admit.

"Guess you could say that," she replied. Curious, she tugged her brows together, mirroring his expression in her own fashion. "Why do you ask?"

His gaze shifted, and he tipped his bearded chin over her left shoulder. She spun in his indicated direction and froze.

"Hello, Camille."

Rhys stood regally at her bar, dressed in an immaculate white T-shirt and faded jeans, and she stared in disbelief, mouth agape. Out front, there hadn't been any huge crashes to announce his arrival, and she glanced behind him, just to be sure. Everything seemed normal; no patrons wiped spilled drinks off their clothes, nor did the wandering wait staff scramble for mops.

Rhys chuckled sheepishly and shrugged, tucking his hands into his front pockets. "I assure you; nothing has been damaged."

"Oh." The ringing bell behind her had snapped her scattered focus. "One second, *cher.*" She quickly turned and, grabbing the hot plate, slid it in front of the chattering patrons off to her right.

"Make sure he don't break nothing, *oui?*" Big Rob's stage whisper had garnered more than a few glances from the regular barflies. Cam opened her mouth to respond, but the man had already vanished back into the depths of the kitchen.

She worked on her game face and returned to the bar. Rhys had slipped into one of the open stools and waited patiently, an air of formality clinging to his glamour as he rested his folded hands neatly on the dark wood. Was he waiting for her to make the first move? *Remember, it was you who kicked him out.*

"Didn't think I'd—"

"You look well," he interjected, the superficial comment designed to be non-threatening. A decent icebreaker, though nothing of any note would be said with so many curious eyes watching their exchange. She relaxed a hair but remained on guard.

"*Merci, cher.*" Another long second passed in the awkward silence before she called to her boss in the kitchen, "Rob, you mind if—"

"Go on, *chère.* 'Sides, don't think I ain't noticed you been working with no breaks. Again."

Cam hoped Rhys would miss her boss unexpectedly outing her, but the stunned widening of his deep topaz eyes told otherwise. She mumbled an incoherent thanks and ducked beneath the gate. Without saying a word, Rhys followed her as she wove through the light crowd. The band was on break, leaving available the booth next to the massive speakers. The intermission between sets was like a makeshift alarm clock, giving her enough time to say what she needed to say.

She motioned to the open seat and slid into the opposite bench, where she waited for Rhys to join her. "So," she said, "guess everything worked out, *oui?*"

Rhys nodded, a hesitant smile touching his lips. "Yes, thanks to you. The supply of antidote you took from the facility has saved all those infected, and the Arch Knight, the highest in my order, learned much from the interaction between the toxin and the cure. From the deep study, he..."

His voice faded as she waved off the continued explanation. She chuckled weakly. "Science was never my strong suit, *cher*."

Rhys laughed and rested his hands on the table.

"So, sounds like you still got your job, non?" At the simple question, he beamed and bobbed his head. An awkward silence enveloped the booth. Cam gnawed on her bottom lip and twisted her loose hair around her fingers. She studied the ring stains on the worn wood and traced the initials carved into the grain by some lovers who knew how many years ago. Were they still together? Had fate given the pair their happily ever after?

A hand covered hers and stilled her fidgeting digits. Huffing out a heavy breath, Cam drew her gaze back to her companion.

"I know you requested to be left alone," he said, "but ... but I wanted to ... to know if—" He paused as if the reason for his surprise visit was entirely on the up and up. "Camille ... are you all right?" His honest concern echoed in his simple question.

She'd missed his sincerity.

Unable to hold back, she shook her head as a sting of tears burned her eyes. "Not really," she squeaked out, masking her grief with a pitiful, strangled laugh. "Just ask anyone here." With a break in the tension, Cam eased back, but not so far that she slipped out of his light touch.

"I ... I have missed you, Camille." A hint of the Rhys she remembered welled up in his heartfelt words, and she wiped away her tears as a relieved smile warmed his face. "I was becoming quite content with the state of our non-physical relationship."

Cam shook her head and chuckled. "Y'all got a strange way of saying friendship there, *cher*."

"Friendship is not a concept valued by my people," he admitted. "But I would be honored to be considered as your friend." He slipped his hand away and placed it reverently over his heart. She'd seen him do this before, and to her, the gesture spoke of chivalrous deeds and honored promises. *Well, he is a knight, after all.*

As she regarded him dressed in standard attire, she realized how much the title suited him; he oozed the strength of myth, and definitely possessed the heart of a hero.

The speakers crackled and popped as the band plugged in their guitars and prepped for their next set. Soon, it would be too loud to even hear herself think. She tilted her head back toward the open dance floor and slid out of the booth, waiting for Rhys to join her. Then she tucked her thumbs into her back pockets and shrugged.

"I gotta be gettin' back to work now." Moment of truth, and she floundered for words. A weight had been lifted from her shoulders, her heart beating a little easier. She stuck out her hand.

Rhys glanced down at her extended palm, and as his gaze returned to hers, a much-missed smile lit up his face. He accepted her offer and, with a simple tug, pulled her into a warm embrace. She wrapped her arms around his midsection and fell into his comforting hug. A strange tingle marched along her skin for just a second. At first, she thought it was a jolt of static electricity, but her body soaked up the additional magical kick, and she hid her smile beneath his armpit.

The music started, an impromptu, sappy ballad. Cam frowned and glared around Rhys at the guys on the stage, while peals of raucous laughter rang out over the tender tune. She chuckled, flipping off the band, and stepped out of Rhys's arms.

"Later, cuz. Give my love to the family, *oui?*"

She'd spoken purposefully louder than normal, hoping her use of the colloquial familial term would dispel any germinating rumors. With a couple of well-placed but disappointed groans, she knew she'd hit her target. She clapped him on his biceps, then gave him a parting nod.

Rhys took the hint and inclined his head toward her. He did know how to make her feel like a princess. She smirked, the dimmed lights hiding her blush, and she watched as he deftly wove his way toward the front doors. Monica, present during Rhys's first visit, guarded her boobs with her empty tray and scurried out of his path.

With a renewed spring in her step, Cam headed back to her bar, a crooked grin firmly cemented onto her lips, and as she moved to duck beneath the gate, a hand grasped her wrist. She froze once again, glancing over her shoulder, shocked by her own eyes and ears as she heard:

"I think I'd like that drink now."

CHAPTER 28

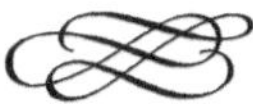

Zacarias had watched, hidden by the long shadows, as Rhys and Camille danced clumsily around their reunion. He'd been observing her for the past two evenings, remaining close, yet honoring her wish for space. He could only stand by as she struggled with her troubling emotions; with each passing hour, he saw her vacillate between moments of forced happiness, and private, all-encompassing grief.

As he was the partial cause for her current distress, he lingered near enough to hear her every word, yet far enough to remain safely out of sight. His magicks had allowed him to easily read her projected turmoil, though he was powerless to remove her heavy burden. By all rights, he should have come to her after the first night to inform her of their success. The serum, administered by the knights in Rhys's order, had not only healed all those infected, but had also armed his kin with the ability to resist any further exposure to the lethal toxin. The queen had heaped high praises upon Zacarias, declaring him the savior of the hour. He reminded her of the contributions of others, however, namely both Rhys and Camille. At the mention of his skin dancer, his pulse had quickened, and an unaccustomed heat had warmed his cheeks.

Luck had been on his side that day and Tannequil had misread his response as anger for having to share the honors with those thought to be beneath the court. Manners dictated all involved be properly acknowledged, and he had been sent to retrieve Camille. But even knowing the feisty halfling would refuse at all odds, he'd graciously accepted his latest task, if only to see her once again.

The second part of the message, however, would be more distasteful to deliver.

Zacarias had remained secreted away, while the sickening and awkward display of emotion had worn on. A part of him hoped she would send him packing. Perhaps then, distraught, she'd have fallen more easily into his arms.

The amiable reconciliation soon ended, giving him the opportunity to make his approach. He halted her before she escaped into the safe zone behind her bar.

The light contact slammed into him, her intoxicating fragrance wafting through the stale air, driving the blood from his brain to below his belt line. Her vibrant green eyes flared wide, and a pale blush warmed her porcelain cheeks. He laced his fingers between hers and guided her to her full height, all the while holding her gaze, basking in the light of her spirit.

A tear clung to her lower lashes, and he wiped it away with the pad of his thumb. The corners of his mouth tugged up the longer he stood close enough to feel the heat from her body, and he trailed his knuckles along her jaw, reveling in her soft skin. A cautious doubt had clouded her eyes, a faint furrow wrinkling the gap between her brows.

"Z-Zacarias? What ... how...?"

She still did not trust him. *Would he?*

If their situations had been reversed, he doubted he'd even allow this moment to occur. She was right to be fearful, especially given his other edict. He nodded, stoic, and eased away from her. He was speechless when she threw her arms around him. A heartbeat passed, and he pulled her in close. Her curves felt like heaven against his body, driving home his hungered need. Burying his face into her silken tresses, he drew her scent into his soul, brushing his lips across the top of her raven hair as he trailed his fingertips along the length of her spine.

Whistles and catcalls ruined the peaceful moment, and he gave her one final squeeze before releasing her. "It seems you have confused your crowd, and they may believe you fickle."

A playful grin tilted her lush lips, and she shook her head. "Nah, *cher*. They're just glad I ain't bawlin' my eyes out every two seconds."

She slipped back under the wooden bar gate and found some menial task with which to occupy her hands. As he watched the delicate choreography, however, he changed his tune. There was nothing common about how she handled her duties—she spun and whirled, skirting around her fellow employees in the narrow alley behind the wooden barrier, sliding drinks and steaming dishes before her clients. A light bounce long absent from her step had returned, as did the cheerful glow in her radiant aura.

"Beer sound good?"

A tall glass of a deep amber brew appeared before him, and he arched a brow, pleased by her choice. She danced away before he could thank her.

He glanced up and down the bar, using his powers covertly.

Human minds were so easy to manipulate, and he had an important message to deliver. As he sipped the flowery malted beverage, he influenced the other patrons, reminding them of imaginary events needing their immediate attention elsewhere.

A few moments later, the area was empty, leaving Camille oddly unoccupied. She swiveled her head, searching the length of the long wooden barrier for her charges and, with a fisted hand coming to rest on her hip, she glared at him.

"I do apologize," he stated, dabbing his lips. "Oh, and thank you. The drink is quite tasty. But"—he shifted gears, needing to get to the heart of the matter—"as I am certain Rhys has told you, you are quite the unsung hero of saving the queen as well as the—"

"Did you have to shoo away all my customers to tell me that, *cher*?" Her adorable frown returned, and he wished she was closer, the drive to kiss away her pout growing with each passing second.

Zacarias inclined his head. "No," he said, "but I do need a measure of privacy to tell you the rest."

She stilled, panic flashing in her rich green eyes. "What do you mean 'the rest'?"

He laid his hand, palm up, on the bar and waited until she inched near. Still, a cloud of doubt hung over her head, but she slipped her fingers between his. He shared in the warmth of her spirit, taking strength from her unique gifts.

"I am sorry if I caused you harm, Camille." Who was more surprised by his words: her or him? He swallowed hard and ventured on. "It was never my intention."

A delicate blush pinked her cheeks, and a hint of a smile touched her lips. "Didn't think you did it on purpose."

Standoffish to the core, he surmised. He trailed the pad of his thumb across her captured fingers. "In truth," he said, "it is the last thing on Earth I would do. You ... you have become very special to me, Camille." He dared no more honesty. More could be dangerous—for the both of them. Yet he would risk all for just one kiss. His gaze dipped to her lush mouth, wondering if its softness existed only in his mind.

Knowing once his news had been delivered, this moment may never come again, he leaned over the barrier and pulled her in close. He stared into her darkening pools of jade, then slanted his mouth over hers. He'd anticipated some level of resistance. Instead, she willingly followed, and he traced the seam of her lips, swallowing her needy whimper like sweet wine. Her jaw slipped down, and he eagerly accepted the invitation, desiring to savor every inch. He swept his tongue across hers, enticing her to come out and play.

At the feel of her fingers threading through his hair, he tightened his grip on his magicks. The tender taste of her had fueled his desire for more, much more than this public setting would allow. Blood drained from his brain, trickled below his constricting belt line. Yet she was still innocent in the ways of his people; pure and inexperienced when it came to the sharing of powers, and he did not want to frighten her. So he opted to enjoy the stolen moment, grateful for her gift.

Gradually, he broke their powerful connection and regarded her beneath heavy eyelids. Her welcoming lips remained parted, as if inviting him in for another sample. He grinned, placing one final kiss on the tip of her nose before gently easing back across the bar.

"Am I forgiven?" he asked.

Camille slowly opened her eyes, rings of shimmering emerald visible as mere halos around the passion-darkened black. A sensual half smile teased the corners of her kiss-swollen lips. "Jury's still out on that one. But let's say you're out of the dog house and onto the porch."

"Good." He sighed in momentary relief. "Because I would hate for you to be in poor spirits when you met the queen."

"Excuse me?" She arched a graceful eyebrow, surprise stealing the warmth from her cheeks, and she sank farther into her side of the bar. "When I do what?"

Begrudgingly, he re-donned the mantel of Grand Enforcer and straightened his spine. "It seems our queen wishes to thank you personally for your part in saving the lives of her people, and of her and her daughter in particular."

Camille scowled. "Tell her to send a card like normal folks."

Zacarias shook his head sagely. "An invitation from Tannequil is not something to be dismissed."

"So I've discovered already," she replied, returning to her duties. "Believe I said no before this whole thing began. You know..." She glanced back at him, and he chuckled inwardly, amused by her charmingly frosty glare. "I don't even remember having a choice in the first place."

"I warned her you would be, shall we say, hesitant to accept." He tossed back the dregs of his nearly forgotten drink, but the cooling beverage did little to slake his thirst for another sip from her lips. She was sweetness and fire combined, the mix intoxicating and addictive.

She gave an unladylike scoff. His heart ached to deliver his final piece of good news, and he sent a private prayer to the heavens for her understanding. He gently grabbed her hand, stilling her frenetic scouring.

"Camille? Do you ... can you trust me?" He purposefully kept his hold light, yet her gaze flitted in every direction except his. "When I said you were dear to me, it is true. More, I fear, than I can put into words." She dragged her eyes up to meet his. *Well, it's a start.* Armed with the meager truce, he forged ahead. "You have caught the attention of the Fae High Court, my little skin dancer, and that is not always a good thing. Some of my brethren will try to either manipulate your loyalties or compromise your integrity. I do not ever want you to believe you are alone in my world. I will stand by your side to keep you safe."

She heaved a sigh, a furtive frown tugging at her lips. "As long as it doesn't put you on anyone's radar. Z, I..." Her shoulders drooped, weighed down by her burdensome confusion. He was partially responsible for her distress, yet only her trust would allow him to share the load. "I want to say yes," she conceded, "but I just don't know."

A distant tapping inside his mind demanded the return with her answer—and soon. He cupped her cheek, savoring the lingering warmth of her blush and, with a hesitant smile, he dipped his chin to capture her gaze. She resisted for only a moment before her wandering eyes found his and, heaving an exaggerated sigh, she replied with a timid grin.

"Does this mean I have a chance?" he whispered, and he tucked a stray lock of her thick raven tresses behind her ear, trailing his fingertips along her jawline.

Camille pinned him with a pensive stare, and he could almost see the wheels spinning behind her sparkling eyes. "How 'bout I think on it and get back to you?"

He lifted her hand to his lips, placed a tender kiss in the center of her palm. The heady scent of night-blooming jasmine flowers and exotic spices filled his senses, cementing her forever into his heart.

Smiling deviously, he stepped backwards and released his privacy shielding. "We will talk on this more next time."

"Next time, *cher?*" She cocked her head, scooping up a nearby empty crystalline stein.

He continued toward the shadowed hallway leading away from the returning crowds. "Why, the next time the queen calls on you, of course." With one foot in the darkness, he twisted to face her, gave her an impish grin. "Oh, did I forget to mention? As of now, you are handmaiden to the High Court of the Fae. Think of it as a token of Her Majesty's gratitude."

"WHAT!"

Zacarias blew her a kiss, then darted into the hidden pathway a heartbeat before the glass stein hurled toward his head had shattered against the wall.

THE MERRY TURNS OF A SKIN DANCER

You didn't think the antics ended there, did you?

Here is a taste of *The Waltz of the Stilleto-Heeled Fairy*, the second installment to the "Merry Turns of a Skin Dancer" trilogy...

A sensual chill raced along Camille's spine a heartbeat ahead of the wolf whistles and cat calls. After Rhys's appearance, she couldn't be absolutely certain that Zacarias was soon to follow.

But judging by the parting crowds, the Grand Enforcer of the Fae Court had just entered the building. She took a deep breath, forced down her growing anticipation and prepared her best smile.

However, the joyful butterflies in her gut were quickly devoured by spiraling serpents and she fought against the urge to launch herself across the bar. Though whether it was to slap him or the scantily-clad piece of arm candy hanging on his elbow, she would never know.

Dressed to the nines in a kohl black suit, Zacarias strolled cool as a cucumber straight to her while the busty blonde beside him practically jogged to keep up. Her ebony patent-leather, sky-high heels added about half a foot to her runway model height and made her legs appear nearly as long as Camille was tall. A black skirt no wider than a belt covered as much as her panties did and a lemon yellow t-shirt she bought in the child's department left most of her perfectly toned and sun-kissed skin available for all to see. She finished the stripper attire with a longline, bohemian-style lavender lace cardigan. Yet it was her shimmering pearlescent blue eyes that betrayed her immortal blood.

Camille had continued to deny any advance of Zacarias. So why was she so damned jealous now?

AUTHOR NOTES

Thank you for allowing my stories into your life and I hope you stay along for the ride. Without readers like you, my characters would only live in my own imaginations.

If you enjoyed this, or any of my works, I would love to hear from you. Drop me a line, send a DM on social media, or even some kind words on a review can make all the difference for an author.

Keep Believing in Magic!

ACKNOWLEDGEMENTS

The fun thing about being a writer is when new characters decide to just pop in and say hello.

It was about five years ago. Normal sort of day, working on what was at the time my current project, *Star-Crossed Negotiations*. I was in the middle of a scenic pickle; trying to figure out how to get my characters to pick up the pace on getting off the damned planet (standard hiccup point for me—moving from the second act into the third). So anyway, I'm staring at the screen, waiting for Kieran to make a move when I hear this decidedly New Orleans drawl in the back of my mind.

What? A Southern belle in outer space? I know I've written stranger things than that, but this was a new everything. She starts whispering about this bar called Gator Bites and growing up during the French Revolution, and most importantly, about her very unique abilities.

Just like that.

Now, I have a whole new series, a new cast of characters, a

new direction that I'd not considered before. Something a little lighter and more comedic. Still tons of snark and steamy situations, because well, it is still me behind the keys.

So I start jotting down snippets and scenes, and soon enough, I've got a whole book, plus ideas for at least two other stories. Maybe Camille will keep whispering about more tales. Guess I'll just have to wait and see.

To bring this new tale to the light of day, I have to give huge props to my Louisiana connection and my sister from another mister, Ri Lahey. Thanks for making sure all the details were just right. First drinks at Gator Bites are on me.

Thank you to my amazing betas, Elma and Mary Max. Thanks for reading and rereading my troublesome scenes and for helping me round up the voices in my head.

To my cover artist and dear friend, Dani. Thanks for your mad skills and for creating my mischievous characters in all their glory.

As always, to my friends who understand the reasons I have to decline so many offers to hang out, yet still check in to make sure I'm okay, love you all more than chocolate and that's saying a lot.

To my family, by blood, by marriage, and by choice, thank you for believing in me and in my stories.

To my husband who puts up with my craziness, thank you for taking this wild ride with me. I'm grateful more than you know to have you at my side.

And to my mom and my dad, watching from the other side of the Veil, I thank you for giving me the strength to follow my heart, and the courage to pursue my dreams.

～

NEVER MISS A NEW RELEASE OR SALE!

Be sure to sign up for my newsletter at www.TessaMcFionn.com

Connect with me!

www.TessaMcFionn.com

tessa@tessamcfionn.com

Instagram: @tessam2112

Threads: @tessam2112

ABOUT THE AUTHOR

Tessa McFionn has always had a love of all things unreal. Growing up reading Tolkien, Heinlein, and comic books, playing D&D, and watching *Thundarr the Barbarian* on Saturday mornings, she was immersed in worlds of magic. When her mother introduced her to *Dune* and *An Interview with a Vampire*, she was hooked on romance in speculative fiction, and after discovering Sherrilyn Kenyon, she realized love can share center stage in the story.

A very native Californian, calling Southern California home for most of her life, she grew up in San Diego and attended college in Northern California and Orange County, only to return to San Diego to work as a teacher. Insatiably curious and imaginative, she loves to learn and discover, making her wicked knowledge of trivial facts an unwelcome guest at many Trivial Pursuit boards.

The Guardians

Spirit Fall, Book One

Spirit Bound, Book Two

Spirit Song, Book Three

Spirit Shattered, Book Four

The Rise of the Stria

To Discover A Divine, Book One

Divine Challenges, Book Two

A Divine's Retribution, Book Three

A Curse of Forever, a supernatural novella

Star-Crossed Negotiations